DEATH STALKS A LADY

After the death of her father, Judith Allen travels across the Atlantic to join the rest of her estranged family in the UK. Upon arrival, she discovers a dead woman in the garage of her mother's house, and is soon thrown into a whirlwind of adventure. As she tries to turn to her family for comfort, the people close to her start dropping like flies in mysterious circumstances. Judith is determined to follow the clues and unmask a murderer. But who can she trust?

Books by Shelley Smith
in the Linford Mystery Library:

THE LORD HAVE MERCY
COME AND BE KILLED
THIS IS THE HOUSE
THE CELLAR AT No.5
BACKGROUND FOR MURDER

SHELLEY SMITH

◆

DEATH STALKS A LADY

Complete and Unabridged

LINFORD
Leicester

First published in Great Britain

First Linford Edition
published 2018

*A catalogue record for this book is available
from the British Library.*

ISBN 978–1–4448–3565–6

Published by
F. A. Thorpe (Publishing)
Anstey, Leicestershire

Set by Words & Graphics Ltd.
Anstey, Leicestershire
Printed and bound in Great Britain by
T. J. International Ltd., Padstow, Cornwall

This book is printed on acid-free paper

PART ONE

1

The Corpse in the Car

I kissed Bob good-bye at the bottom of the lane, because I didn't want him to come any farther with me. I only kissed him because he looked so pathetic, with mournful brown eyes like my spaniel, when I had to leave her behind. I was sorry Bob Stone was that way about me, for he really was rather sweet. So I promised to write, and watched the car slide away out of sight. Then I picked up my valise and started up the lane.

I could see the top of our old house on the rise of the hill. I remembered the outline of it against the sky. I felt strange and sad and home-sick, all at once. As I walked slowly up the lane I noticed a few new houses, a tiny green-and-white bungalow, some converted cottages, here and there.

I turned in at the drive and paused. It

was as lovely as I remembered, a gracious old house, its sturdy lines veiled now in creeper. When we built the garage Father put it down by the gates so as not to spoil the shape of the house. I was standing by the garage now, and I could hear a faint throbbing inside which roused me from my contemplation.

Curious, I walked round the garage and opened the door. It was dim inside but I could discern the bulk of a car, its engine racing. I walked forward. Something was folded over the steering-wheel. I rapped sharply on the glass, and then jerked open the door, the driver's side. I hadn't expected it to open. The thing inside toppled out very slowly across my feet. Even in the darkness I could see the pale gold hair tumbled upside-down as her hat slid off.

The next thing was I was back on the roadway and somebody was yelling, and it was me. I was very ashamed of that when I realized it. I was hooting like a locomotive, with boiled macaroni for legs, and altogether looking every inch the heroine, I *don't* think. I wished now I had let Bob stay with me as he wanted.

What I would have done next, goodness only knows. But someone said gently in my ear, 'What is the matter, my dear? Have you been stung or bitten by something?'

The voice belonged to a man wearing a panama hat, but I was too upset to notice more than that he was sunburnt and attractive. I caught hold of his arm and began to blubber out something about a dead body. He cut me short by asking sharply where. I said, 'In the car, there.' So he said hadn't we better go and look, because it might not be dead at all. I led the way reluctantly, wishing I didn't feel so swimmy inside.

When we got inside, he said, 'Wait there.' He felt about for the light switch, and turned it up. Then he walked round the side of the car and stood looking down at the girl for a moment. He stuck his head inside the car, and drew it out again pretty smartly. There was a fearful stink, because all this while the engine had been running. He fumbled around and brought out a hanky and, leaning across the body again and into the car, switched off the engine. There was a blessed silence. He put the hanky back in his pocket, and bent over the dead girl without touching her. She was lying awkwardly, her body twisted down from the driver's seat, across the running-board, with head and shoulders resting uncomfortably on the garage floor. The ends of her fair hair sprawled into a dirty patch of oil. From where I stood she looked quite young and rather pretty. She was wearing a little blue linen suit, and I guessed she had blue eyes too.

The man in the panama hat touched her cheek with the back of his hand, and shook his head. He stood up and came over and took me by the elbow. 'Let's go,' he said. 'There's nothing we can do.'

'Couldn't we — do something to make her more — more comfortable?'

'Better leave it all just as it is, my dear, until the police have seen it.' He steered me out.

We walked down the lane, and he was still holding me by the elbow, as if he feared I might run away.

'Where are we going? To the police? 'I asked presently.

'No, we'll see if the mountain won't come to Mahomet for once. I need a drink, and I daresay you do too.'

He led me across to the little white bungalow I had noticed on my way up. The living-room was full of sunlight and well furnished. He pushed me down into a deep lounge chair and ordered me with firm kindness to stay there and relax till he came back.

'I'm not going to ask you what you want to drink,' he said, 'because a young lady of your age ought not to know.'

I laughed. 'I'll take what I get, and like it.'

He brought back a large rye for himself and a small one for me. While I gulped at it, he used the telephone. The rye soon braced me up again. The man smiled across at me while he waited for his connection. Now that he had removed his hat, I could see that he had dark wavy hair, faintly grey at the temples. His teeth looked very white against his tanned face when he smiled. He was awfully well dressed too. And that reminded me — I flipped open my compact and groaned with despair: my hair was all over the place.

He turned at my groan and inquired what the trouble was. I tugged the comb viciously through my tangled curls.

'I look the picture of a heroine, don't I?' I said disgustedly.

'You look sweet to me,' he said. And then, into the 'phone, 'Put me through to the sergeant, please. Hurry, don't argue.'

When he had finished talking he replaced the receiver with a sigh. 'Now, suppose we introduce ourselves,' he suggested, proffering me his open cigarette-case. 'I am Rex Brady — very much at your disposal, madam.'

'How do you do, Mr. Brady. I am Judith Allen — '

'Oh-ho. So you're Judith Allen? I'd never have known it. You don't take after your family, do you? Or — yes, perhaps you are a little like Millicent, come to think of it.'

I jumped to my feet. 'A fine daughter I am. I'd clean forgotten all about them. I guess they'll be worrying themselves into fits because I haven't turned up. I'd better go right away before they send for the bloodhounds. Thanks most awfully for everything . . . ' I was half out of the door when he hauled me back.

'Oh no, you don't,' he said. 'This is your party too. You stay put till the police have heard your story, my dear. But you needn't worry about your family, as it happens, they're not in. They've gone to meet you.'

I frowned. 'But I didn't see them at the docks. Could we have missed one another?'

'Would you recognize them if you saw them?'

'I guess so,' I said dubiously.

'Another explanation might be that you are not Judith Allen at all.'

'Well, of all the — ' I said indignantly.

He smiled gently. 'What time did you berth?'

I faltered out that it was about 8.30 a.m., and I had cleared the customs in a couple of hours.

'And what train did you catch?'

'I came by car,' I said sulkily. 'A friend of mine . . . dropped me at the bottom of the lane. I made him go. I wish I hadn't now.'

'Pass, friend,' he said cheerfully. 'I'm glad you're the real McCoy, as they say over your side.'

And then the sergeant and a police constable came in. After they had sorted themselves out, I found that the sergeant had gone up to the garage with Mr. Brady and left me to take care of the policeman. He was young and fair, with a smooth baby face, and he stood by the door, hands behind his back.

'Won't you sit down, Constable?' I said sweetly.

He refused politely, studiously avoiding my eyes. I rubbed my lipstick off and painted on a nice fresh mouth.

Presently the two men returned. The sergeant 'phoned up the station and handed out a few cryptic orders; he wanted the police-van to take the body to the mortuary and the police surgeon to be notified, the limousine to be removed from the garage, and a whole lot more besides. Then he sent Babyface along to the garage.

'Now then,' said the sergeant briskly, and drew a small pad out of his pocket. 'Suppose we hear the young lady's story first. Will you tell me just in your own words, Miss — '

'I only landed this morning, from America,' I said. 'An acquaintance I made on board insisted on driving me as far as here. Actually, I left him at the bottom of the lane and walked up alone. When I got to the garage I could hear an engine throbbing and it seemed to come from there, and I went to have a look.'

'Did it seem suspicious to you?'

'I don't know that I thought about it at all. I just went to look.'

'Feminine curiosity,' muttered Mr. Brady, and his eyes twinkled at me.

I ignored him. 'I opened the garage door, and walked over to the car. I could see someone huddled over the wheel. I tapped on the glass, but she didn't move. Then I — I opened the door and she — fell right out on me,' I gulped.

'Quite,' said the sergeant. 'And then

what happened?'

'I guess I shot out of there pretty quick. The next thing I remember is standing in the lane screaming. And then Mr. Brady happened along — '

'Just a minute, please,' said the sergeant. 'Would you mind telling me what brought you on the scene, sir?'

'Well, Sergeant, I was about to indulge in a siesta when this young lady's excellent vocal powers advised me that valour, for a man of parts, is better any day than discretion. What more could any knight-errant ask? I went to her assistance, naturally. Together we returned to the garage. The place was foul with carbon monoxide. I switched off the engine, being careful to use a handkerchief in order not to spoil any fingerprints. Then I looked at the poor girl; and even to my inexperienced eye she was quite unmistakably dead. There didn't seem to be anything we could do. And I thought it best to leave everything undisturbed as far as possible. Then I escorted the young lady back here and rang up the police station and notified you. I think that's all . . . '

'Have you ever seen the deceased before?'

'No; not that I remember, anyway.'

'And you, Miss?'

'I'm a stranger in these parts.'

'Ah, yes, of course. You only landed today from America?' He smiled faintly. 'Would you mind going back, Miss, to when you came up the lane in the first place. You were passing the garage, heard the engine running, went into someone else's garage to — '

'I wasn't *passing* the garage, I was standing in the drive just beside it.'

'Why?'

'I was looking at the house, of course, admiring it and thinking how little it had changed — '

'Ah,' he interrupted triumphantly, 'then you *have* been here before. Why did you say you were a stranger in these parts?'

'Why, that's only a wisecrack — '

'So you might have seen the dead girl before.'

'I've just told you, I haven't. You don't think I'm lying to you, do you?'

'Of course not, Miss! I only wanted to get things straight for the report. Now, what did you say your name was, Miss?'

'I didn't say, but no matter. I'm Judith Allen.'

'Judith Allen!' The sergeant's jaw dropped.

Mr. Brady said, 'I thought I noticed rather a resemblance myself, but it might be only a similarity of build and colouring, they're both blonde and I should judge about the same height. Nothing more to it than that.'

The policeman said stolidly, 'What would you be alluding to, sir?'

Mr. Brady didn't answer.

'Are you by any chance related to the Mrs. Allen of Elder Hall?' said the sergeant, turning to me again.

'She's my mother,' I said impatiently.

'Oh!' He looked relieved. 'That accounts for why you said you had seen it before then.'

Ridiculous man, I thought. 'Obviously you are not local,' I said pretty tartly, 'or you would know that I didn't leave these parts till I was ten.'

'And is this the first time you've been back since then? Not a very nice welcome for you, Miss . . . And were your family aware that you were returning, or was it to be in the nature of a surprise?'

'I told them; what do you think? I'm no black sheep to have to spring it on them suddenly.'

He laughed deprecatingly. 'Well, I expect you are glad to be back in the old country once more, eh? And I'm sure your family will be just as glad to have you with them again, a nice bright young lady like you.' He paused.

'And there's this other young lady, just about your own age, cut off in the bud of her life,' he continued poetically. 'I wonder what she was doing in your mother's garage?'

'Search me. She might be a friend, I suppose. Poor kid! How did it happen, do you think?' I felt it was my turn to ask a question.

'We shall know more when we have the police surgeon's report,' he said noncommittally.

'I suppose,' I mused, 'she must have felt

a bit queer and driven in there and fainted before she could switch off the engine, and then — '

'You think she was overcome by the fumes of carbon monoxide?'

'I just took it for granted. I mean, I've often read in the papers, back in the States, of folks dying that way.'

'Have you now, Miss — er — Allen, that's very interesting. It opens up fields of speculation.'

'On the other hand,' said Mr. Brady, 'it would be an unusual way to commit suicide.'

'Suicide!' I swung round.

'That remark was merely to keep the pot boiling, my child.'

'Do *you* think so?' I asked the policeman.

'I should be wary of venturing to give an opinion,' he said cautiously. 'The brief examination I have made of the contents of her bag proved very interesting though. Oh yes. It would be useful if we knew, for instance, why she was passing under the name of Judith Allen!'

2

Who Was Judith Allen?

'Judith Allen,' I gasped. 'You're crazy. There must be some mistake.'

'One would think so, wouldn't one?'

'Surely it is too much of a coincidence to have two Judith Allens right on the same spot at the same time.'

The sergeant scratched his head. 'Now that is just what I am wondering. And that obviously alters the whole conception.'

'I suppose you haven't got a twin anywhere about that you happen to have forgotten?' suggested Brady.

'If I had, we wouldn't have both the same name, my dear man. Are you sure of the name, Sergeant?'

'She had letters addressed to her in her bag, and a handkerchief, marked J.A.'

'Can I have a look at her again?' I got to my feet. 'I think I may be able to show you something. No, I'm not going to tell you what it is, in case I'm mistaken.'

'I don't see why not,' the policeman said, looking at Mr. Brady.

Brady frowned at me. 'Do you think you ought to, Judith? It's not a very pleasant sight for a young girl.'

I looked at him scornfully. 'Pleasant, of course it's not pleasant. Who said it was? I never expected *you* to be so old-fashioned. Let's get cracking.'

She was lying there down at the station covered with a sheet, her limbs composed straightly. The policeman pulled the sheet away from her face. I could feel him watching me as I looked at her. There was a certain resemblance, I suppose; we might have passed for sisters at a pinch. But it looked as if her hair had known a bleach, now that I had clear daylight on it. Animated, I guessed she would pass as pretty.

But it wasn't her face that was going to tell me anything. Her bag was by her side, but empty now. It was cheap imitation leather, and with no maker's name inside. Bracing myself, I leant forward and grabbed her slipper by the heel and jerked it off her foot. I gave it the once over and smiled. I felt pretty smart, showing the professionals how to do it.

'Take a peek at that,' I said, handing the shoe to the sergeant. 'See . . . there's the name Treadwell inside, an English make. And now look at mine.' I slipped it off. 'Hand-made, American cut, Fifth Avenue shop. This girl may be called Judith Allen, but it doesn't look as if she is me, does it?'

The sergeant nodded grudgingly. 'That leaves us an English Judith Allen to trace. Very much obliged to you, Miss, I'm sure. Well, I think that's all then.' He conducted us to the door and then, just as we were going, said: 'Can you suggest any reason why anyone should wish to impersonate you?'

But I was feeling huffy myself by then, and I said, 'No. How should I? Let me know how you get on, my good man.'

'You're a card, young Judith,' chuckled Mr. Brady, as soon as we were out of earshot. 'Saucing policemen!'

'I wasn't going to tell him. None of his business.'

He gave me that sort of English look

19

that Ronald Colman gives you — quizzical, rather fascinating.

'Whew!' he exclaimed. 'I'm fair wore out. That's old age creeping on, Judith, and there are you as fresh as a cucumber.'

'You're not old, Mr. Brady.'

'Oh, don't call me Mr. Brady — after all we have been through together. Call me Uncle Rex.'

'Not *Uncle*! But I'll call you Rex, if you like.'

He bowed courteously. 'I hope you'll let me be a kind of honorary uncle to you, since I'm a friend of the family.'

'Oh, are you?'

'Well, of your brother's really. Terry and I have painted the town very red once or twice. He's a great chap.'

'Yes? I don't remember him very well. He was mostly at school.'

'You'll like him,' he promised me.

'I expect I'll be seeing them all pretty soon now, won't I?'

'Shy?' He squeezed my arm reassuringly. 'I'll go up to the house with you.'

A car flashed past us and topped the rise.

'You've been awfully kind,' I said. 'Really, when I think of all the things you've done for me already — '

'Oh, we're old friends, aren't we? I won't send in a bill just yet.'

I was silent for a while, thinking. Then I said, 'I suppose if you're a friend of the family you know about — about Father.'

'Yes.' He patted my shoulder.

We didn't speak any more. When we turned in at the drive, the dark limousine that had passed us a while back was standing before the house. Two women stood on the broad steps arguing. They walked up towards the open front door.

Rex called, 'Millicent . . . ' And waited for her to turn and come back towards him. 'Here's your young daughter,' he added, pushing me forward. 'Found her wandering around, and kept an eye on her till you turned up.'

Millicent was as big as I remembered her, and very fair. In spite of her bulk, she had a very graceful way of floating over the ground.

'My baby,' she said, and held out her arms to me. I kissed her. She said,

'Goodness, how you've grown! I'm awfully glad you aren't wearing mourning, darling. Antonia said I ought to, but it's not as though your father had been anything to me for years.'

'Oh, I don't think he'd expect it,' I said awkwardly.

'There you are, Toni, you hear that? He was a very reasonable man — in some ways. It's not that I have any objection to wearing black. Being so very fair I look superb in it. It's the hypocrisy . . . '

'Oh, do shut up, Mother. How you go on and on . . . '

The tall dark girl came towards us, frowning. She was very attractive, with her short sleek hair with dark chestnut lights in it, and her large green eyes that looked light in her brown face. She looked a bit like Father, only more bad-tempered. She wore her clothes carelessly, a short-sleeved scarlet sweater with a grey flannel skirt and brogues.

'This is your sister Antonia,' said our mother.

'She hasn't changed so much, you know,' said Antonia, coolly staring at me and through me.

'Oh, come, I was half this high and had braids and a bang last time,' I said laughingly, and held out my hand.

She raised an eyebrow. 'Braids and a bang! What a little Yankee!'

'Plaits and a fringe, then,' I said, flushing. She had ignored my hand, and I hoped she was going to like me.

Millicent tucked my hand under her arm.

'Don't pay any attention to that silly girl. Come on up to the house, dear. Will you come in and have a drink, Rex?' she called over her shoulder.

Rex waved his hand. 'No, I won't intrude on the family reunion — a sacred moment. See you all later.'

'Good-bye, Rex,' I shouted, 'and thanks a lot.'

I felt as though my last friend was gone and I was alone among strangers.

' . . . Can't think how we missed you.' Millicent was talking. 'Did you get off on the first tender or the second? It was drizzling when we arrived . . . It would, of course, at Liverpool — '

'Liverpool!' I exclaimed. 'But what made you think I was arriving there? I docked at Southampton this morning.'

'Well, naturally,' said Antonia. 'I knew you would arrive at Southampton, but I couldn't nail it into Mother's head, the dear little scatterbrain. She insisted on Liverpool. She'd worked it out from the stars or something.'

We walked into the hall panelled with dim, time-polished wood.

'Now that's a curious thing,' said Millicent. 'When I cast the house yesterday, Saturn was over cardinal. That was a warning of trouble. I couldn't think what it could be at the time. I can't think how I came to be so stupid. Poor Judith, I expect you're tired out. I'll take you to your room right away, and you can have a wash and a rest. Are you interested in astrology, dear?'

I admitted that I didn't know anything about it.

'Oh, Mother will soon teach you,' said Antonia, trailing up the stairs behind us.

'Toni is a disbeliever,' Millicent explained. 'She disbelieves everything, on

24

principle. Poor child, it makes life so dull for her. But there, when she's my age she'll be glad enough to believe that she isn't solely master of her fate. If only I had been more sensible yesterday about the warning . . . '

'Well, if you had avoided it, the stars wouldn't have been true, would they?' said Toni.

Before Millicent could answer, I cut in: 'Oh yes, they would. Trouble came in another way, too.' I drew in a breath, watching them. 'A girl was found in your garage — dead.'

'But how terrible! And what a peculiar place . . . ' my mother chattered. Toni said nothing.

In my little white bedroom with its hangings sprayed with apple blossom, I sat down on the bed and told it to them as well as I was able. The only thing I held back — and I'm not sure that I know why I did that — was that the girl's name was Judith Allen. I let them think they hadn't traced who she was yet. I didn't believe for a moment that really was her name. Antonia's face was softer when I had finished my recitation. 'Poor kid,' she said, meaning me, 'what a rotten beginning.' Millicent wanted to ask more questions, but Toni headed her off by reminding her that someone called Neville was coming to dinner.

'Would you like yours in bed, Judy?'

'Why, no. I'll take a shower, if I may, and freshen up a bit.'

'Not shower,' said Toni. 'Bath. Don't bother to change. Neville isn't anyone, just the bailiff. He's got a crush on Mother.'

They'd had the bathroom done up since my day. It was all pink tiles and glass now. And they'd had the great beams in the ceiling stripped, and they toned in with it surprisingly well. I wondered what the ghost thought about it. Yes, of course there is a ghost attached to Elder Hall. Can you imagine a house this old not having one? But no one has ever seen it that I know of. Though we once had a cook who swore that she had walked slap through it — a tall moaning man, she said; but we never believed that story because she drank.

I found a pink jar of verbena crystals and flung some in the bath. It smelt sweet and steamy and familiar, and I lay there trying not to be a baby. But I missed Dad awfully. He'd only been dead a month, and at first there was so much for me to see to that I hardly noticed he was gone. But now there was nothing more for me to do, and I could relax and feel it. I felt homesick. Would England ever seem like home to me again? Would I get used to these cold, clipped voices? Would my family ever seem like my very own? I reminded myself sternly that I was English through and through and that living in the States didn't make it my country — this was my country. I remembered how often the kids had made me cry at school by calling me 'Limey!' I could hardly expect my mother to act as if she were crazy to see me when she had had to get on without me for nearly ten years. It was pretty decent of her to have me back at all, come to think of it. It was a darling thing to have cabled me to come over when she heard that Father was dead.

She looked kind-hearted. And maybe Antonia would be friendlier presently. I wondered when I was going to see my brother Terence, and what he would be like. All told, I would have given a lot to have some frank, open-hearted American like — like — well, Bob Stone, for instance — right beside me. Not right at that moment, of course. The notion of Bob's embarrassment tickled me, and I laughed and sat up and began lathering myself briskly. Somewhere a gong vibrated dully . . .

I hurried over my dressing, but I needn't have bothered, for when I eventually went down no one was there yet. I opened one of the doors cautiously and peered inside, feeling rather like Bluebeard's wife. It was a small room lined with books on three of the walls and a strip of casement windows running along the width of the fourth. The library evidently. I went over to look at the books. Rows of uniformly bound classics, two incomplete editions of different encyclopaedias, some paper-backed foreign books, and carelessly stacked heaps of modern novels in their bright jackets. I picked up one at random.

'Hullo, hullo, hullo! Who have we here?' said a jaunty voice behind me.

I turned to see an old man — well, fiftyish — standing there in his tuxedo, looking the typical Englishman. The hangdog-plumber-cum-old public-schoolboy type. You know, lean and averagely tall, with a long nose and a fishy eye; you can see hundreds of them decorating the pages of the illustrated papers, sitting on shooting-sticks at the races. This one had pepper and salt hair and a sandy moustache. When he smiled at me I could see that he had a snag tooth. There was something, I thought, very faintly familiar about his face.

I said, 'Hello! I'm Judith Allen. How do you do?'

'The devil you are!' he exclaimed. 'So you managed to get here after all. Plucky girl! Well, I don't know about you, but I could do with a sun-downer, a nice stiff one,' he said, tugging energetically at a bell-rope. A maid came in bearing bottles and glasses on a salver. 'Ah,' he said, rubbing his hands together, 'that's the stuff.' He poured out the drinks and brought mine across to me. 'Jove,' he said admiringly, having apparently noticed me for the first time, 'you certainly take after your mother in looks. By the way, I don't think I introduced myself. I'm Neville Thompson. I look after the estate for your mother, you know. It needs — '

The door burst open and Millicent, in filmy grey chiffon, floated mistily towards us. ' . . . Poor lambs, you've been waiting. Have you two got acquainted? Angel, pour me a very small drink.'

Neville bowed over her hand.

'What do you think of my brand-new daughter, Neville?' She pulled me towards her.

'A sight for sore eyes. I have just paid her the great compliment of telling her that she favoured you.'

'Judy, you don't want to pay any attention to him, he's a cunning old flatterer. We won't wait dinner for Toni. She's probably forgotten all about it and is sitting down in her briefs to work out an idea that has suddenly come to her. Poor Toni!' She laughed.

'Oh I say, Dancing Lady collapsed at the post, old girl. I'm awfully sorry,' Neville said apologetically.

'That really is sickening.' Millicent looked annoyed.

'I've got a hunch for a double tomorrow.'

'Oh, your hunches! It's too foolish for words to gamble in that haphazard way. One must be scientific and logical about it. Of course, you think it's all just a matter of luck, pure chance, but you're wrong. If the horoscopes are cast correctly there can't be any mistake. I would never have backed Dancing Lady on your judgment alone, only I had mislaid Wragg's horoscope. It's too annoying, people are so careless with little bits of paper, they just throw them away without bothering to see if it's of any importance.' She swept through the door and we followed behind meekly.

When we were halfway through the second course, Antonia strode in, dark, sulky and handsome in a bright plaid taffeta housecoat. She sat down without a word.

Neville asked me civil questions about the trip over, and whether I was glad to be back, and if I remembered England. Why, ten years was half a lifetime; of course I remembered. When I came to think of it, I had spent as much of my young life with Mother as I had with Dad. Then why, I wondered, was Mother's memory so dim, so unreal compared with him? I wondered, too, seeing Mother sitting at the head of the table so elegantly, why they had ever separated. It wasn't a thing Father would ever talk about. Probably, it was what they call incompatibility of temperament. And then, me being the youngest, or perhaps he liked me best, or took me with him because I looked like Millicent — but that would have been painful for him, I should have thought. Father being a Catholic, he would never divorce Mother, which was kind of tough on her in a way; being a pretty woman, she might easily have wanted to get married. On the other hand, there was no reason why she could not have divorced him, I suppose, for desertion or that mouthful about conjugal rights. But she never did, so either she had no reason to or — or — she didn't want to drop the pretty substantial pay-packet Father allowed her. I knew about the separation allowance because Dad always used to grumble about it when the time came round — not that he grudged it her. I don't believe he did one bit, he was too generous-hearted, but he liked to get value for money. I used to tease him about it and say I was the return he got for it, and cheap at the price. Dear Dad! And why should I worry my head about Millicent, she didn't look as if she was fretting, and she'd probably been salting it away for years.

I felt Neville's eyes on me.

'I tell you what, old lady, one of these nights I'm going to sit up with a gun and shoot the first poacher I see, without further warning, damn their eyes. That's a vow. A rabbit or two here or there, that's one thing, but this is daylight robbery. Millicent,' he said, still with his eyes on me, 'doesn't she remind you somehow of my kid. She's a great girl. I'd like you to meet her, Judith, you'd be real pals.' He put his hand on my arm.

'I'm a widower,' he went on, 'and it's been pretty tough on my girlie having no one but her old Dad to guide her. You can understand that, you'd have that in common — '

Antonia leant back in her chair and laughed.

'The soul of tact, as always, Neville. I can hear your thoughts rattle. But it's all right, Judith is pretty smart, she's twigged.'

The situation was saved by Mother rising from the table and guiding us out of the room. I was excusably tired and went to bed early. I refused to think of anything unpleasant and chose to remember instead a happy holiday Dad and I had spent at Miami, a couple of years back. In spite of that I had a beastly nightmare. I dreamt that I had to hurry back to America, and I rushed over to a big, black limousine and pulled open the door — and — and Rex Brady was inside, dead, and he fell out on top of me, and as I tried to push him away his dead mouth began kissing me . . . and I woke up half-suffocated and sweating.

I switched on the light and jumped out of bed. For a moment I couldn't remember where I was. I wanted a drink of iced water badly. But this was England, so of course there wasn't any. I decided to raid the ice-box. I opened the door quietly and stuck my nose out. It was very dark, and I couldn't remember where the switch was. I could hear the wood snapping and creaking, the way it always does in an old house. And then it dawned on me that it wasn't age and atmospherics; it was footsteps, slow and careful. I waited, listening. At the end of the passage was a narrow window; in a moment it was obscured by a dark shape, tall as a man. Then it slipped past the oblong, greyish darkness and was lost. The house was still. My wrist watch told me it was two-thirty a.m. I shivered, and tried to remember the legend of the Elder Hall ghost. I decided to get along without the iced water somehow. I went back to bed and — miraculously — to sleep.

3

I Am Warned

When I came down next morning, I found the breakfast-room empty, but for Millicent, surrounded with sheaves of paper and open books. She didn't look up when I came in but said, 'Darling, when were you born? I simply must do your horoscope. You'd like that, wouldn't you?'

I kissed her good-morning. 'I'd love it,' I laughed. 'But I don't actually remember when I was born. Surely you'd remember that better than I!'

'I suppose I ought to. I know it was half-past four in the morning, but whether it was the third or the fourth, and was it October . . . ? So much has happened since then.'

'You always gave us to understand it was the seventh of September.'

'So it was,' she smiled delightedly.

'How did you sleep, dear?'

I hesitated, and then told her the truth, about my dream and the 'ghost.'

'Poor baby,' she said sympathetically, 'what a horrid dream. I expect you were not properly awake when you thought you saw the ghost.'

I said, 'Of course, I don't believe in ghosts. But I thought perhaps it was Terence, come home late.'

'No,' said Millicent. 'I don't expect him home till the weekend.'

There was a letter for me in an unfamiliar writing. I slit up the envelope, and looked at the signature inside. It was from Bob Stone. Merely a brief note, it said, to wish me happiness in my new home. I thought that was awfully sweet of him. It made me feel cosy, even if he meant nothing to me.

My trunks arrived, and I spent the morning unpacking. Midway, Antonia strolled in and sat herself on the bed, watching me. She lit a cigarette and smoked in silence.

'Well,' she said at last, 'do you think you're going to like it here?'

'That depends a good deal on the people.'

'And how do you like us so far?' she said unpleasantly.

'Goodness, it's early days yet,' I said cheerfully. 'Suppose you tell me a bit more about things. Tell me about Terence.'

'I can't tell you anything about Terry. He's a dark horse, is our brother. Keeps his own counsel.'

'What does he do? What's his job?' I slipped a little grey suit on a wardrobe hanger.

'My dear, Terry has had more jobs than anyone I've ever heard of. Courier, cabaret-artist, explorer, waiter, lorry-driver . . . That's just a few. The last time he spoke of work to me he told me of a scheme he had to stand for Parliament as an independent Anarchist, forming his own party, financed by some wealthy woman or another . . . Don't ask me whether he's still at it or what happened. Crazy! Generally, he hardly comes near this place unless he is in some jam or another. But it's different now. He has a lady friend in the neighbourhood.'

'Oh, someone nice?'

Antonia grimaced. 'Very classy. Not my cup of tea.'

'And Terence is a dark horse and a bit of a — well, a waster, eh?'

'He's been spoilt, that's his trouble. Don't let me put you off him. I thought Father would have told you about him, that's all.'

'Told me what?' I queried.

She glanced at me quickly. 'Let sleeping dogs lie.'

'You started it,' I said crossly. 'Well, you don't seem to have a very high opinion of your family anyway.'

'No,' she agreed equably.

There didn't seem to be any answer to that. The talk shifted to clothes in a careless, disinterested way. I wondered what Antonia *did* care about.

Presently I said, 'Tell me about Rex Brady. What sort of man is he? Is he married, for instance?'

She rolled her eyes at me mockingly. 'A victim already?'

'No. Just curiosity; and he happened to

be rather kind to me, that's all.' But I could feel myself blush.

Toni laughed. 'As it happens, I can't tell you much. So far as I know, he is not married; though how he managed to evade it with his looks I wouldn't know. No one really knows who he is or what he does; he's the local mystery man. He's not a resident, you see. Just down here on a vacation. I think Terry told him about the place. He's a friend of his, if that's any recommendation.'

I signified that I already knew that. 'He was nice to me,' I repeated. 'That's all I know.'

* * *

Rex came up to see me later in the day to inquire how I was. I thought it was awfully thoughtful of him. We went out into the garden and strolled along the alleys of trees. He told me he had been to the police station before coming up to me. They had traced the car that was found in our garage to a Miss Olivia Fane, a lady who lived nearby, just down the lane. Two days before, when she herself had been in London, her car had been stolen while she was shopping in a big store. She had, of course, immediately reported the loss to the Metropolitan Police. They had also traced the dead girl. Her name was Averil Day, and she was an actress of sorts, living alone in rooms Pimlico way.

'Well, that seems to make it more of a muddle than ever,' I said. 'What do you think it all means?'

He shrugged, He looked — sort of puzzled and worried.

'What can she have been doing in a stolen car? And if she knew it was stolen — I mean, if she or an accomplice had stolen it — why on earth did she bring it down here, almost to the real owner's front door? Unless — she was bringing it back. And then, why not right back? Perhaps she was a friend of this lady — Miss Fane?'

'Well, I don't know I'm sure,' said Rex. 'And I don't believe the police do either. Let's talk of something more cheerful. Come down to the village with me and have an icecream.'

I could see no reason to refuse. Rex was awfully interesting. He seemed to have been everywhere and done everything. He told me just one enthralling story after another; it was better than any film. I absolutely hung on his words; I mean, one simply cannot compare mature men of the world with mere callow youths. Boys mean absolutely nothing in my young life. It takes a man of the world to appreciate a girl properly, and not just because she's got long eyes and legs and yellow hair.

And it was while I was listening to Rex as we walked down the village main-street, that I became aware of someone barring my path. And I looked up with a frown to see to my complete amazement Bob Stone grinning down at me a little sheepishly.

'Why, Bob Stone, what in the world are you doing here?' I cried.

'Hullo, Judy,' he said. 'Just thought I'd run along and see how you were making out.'

'Why didn't you let me know, for Pete's

sake? But never mind, you're here now and I'm mighty glad to see you. Rex, this is the boy on the boat I told you about, you know — Bob Stone. Let me introduce you. Mr. Brady, Mr. Stone.'

They shook hands like a couple of strange dogs on leashes. It would have been funny except that when men look at one another like that it always makes me go squingy inside, it's so uncivilised. They always look as though they're going to tear out each other's throats in another minute. Not that I think I'm any Helen of Troy, it just happens to be the way men act.

Rex said disapprovingly, 'You're very young, Mr. Stone . . . much younger than I imagined . . . '

'But I told you he was only a boy,' I said.

'Eh? Oh yes, so you did,' he smiled at me absently.

'I'm twenty-three, Mr. Brady,' said Bob seriously.

'I still think that is too young.'

'Too young for what?' I cried.

'Oh,' said Rex, with a vague smile. 'For

— for marriage, say.'

'Well, that depends how old the girl is, surely,' said Bob, twinkling at me.

I could feel myself blushing furiously as the two of them turned to look at me critically. They *were* mad!

'What an *idiotic* conversation,' I said. Bob shifted awkwardly from one foot to the other, looking from me to Rex and back to me again. Maybe when I am older I shall be able to handle those situations deftly, but all that I could think of was to dive into one of those crazy little village stores that manage to stock everything. I wanted some nail varnish, and they even managed to produce some of that. I hung about and bought some candy and a few odds and ends of haberdashery, as you call it over here. When I came out into the street the two men had gone.

Then I saw them walking slowly towards me and talking. Evidently they had strolled up the street and down again, the way one does, absorbed in conversation. The moment they caught sight of me Bob hurried towards me eagerly. He looked an awful old slouch beside Rex. I couldn't help noticing that. Not that Rex was over-dressed or anything of that sort; his clothes were absolutely right. His tie lay smoothly down his chest in a straight line from beneath his cleft chin, in the rich dark stripes that signified a famous public school; while Bob's gaudy confection, fluttering madly in the breeze, might have graced an Atlantic City Convention. Rex's panama was cool and summery; while Bob had crushed a bright green pork-pie on the back of his brown curls. And so on.

Rex said, 'I'm going to run away, my dear, and leave you with your young friend. I understand he is only here for a few hours, and anyway old friends naturally must come first. Being neighbours, we shall be able to see each other on plenty of other occasions. Thank you very much for giving me the pleasure of your company this morning. And if you both feel like a cocktail later on, well — you know where I live, Judith. Good-bye, Mr. Stone. Glad to have made your acquaintance and hope we may meet again some day.' So suave, so courteous.

'Thank goodness he had the sense to see he wasn't wanted,' said Bob as soon as Rex was out of earshot. 'Come for a run-around in the jalopy, Judy?'

'All right,' I said, not very graciously, 'We'll ride around a while and then I'll take you home; I want to see how you like the Hall.' I climbed into the tattery old car that had been super-chic in 1924. We shot forward, and in a few minutes the village was out of sight.

Fields of wheat, rustling faintly in the breeze, nodded as we flashed past. I removed my hat, and my hair streamed out behind me like a banner. I let the wind bat down my eyelids peacefully. Something was faintly worrying in the back of my mind.

'Say, Bob, had you ever met Mr. Brady before?'

'Why, no, Judy. What makes you ask that?'

'You both acted as if you knew one another,'

'Gosh, no! Never seen him before in my life. Not likely to forget a pansy dial like that in a hurry.'

'He may look a pansy to a tough guy like you,' I said bitingly, 'but there's nothing cissy about him, I promise you. I know because we were in a nasty spot together, and gosh did he have *poise!*'

'Sorry,' said Bob tightly. 'Didn't know I was speaking of one of your pets. Thought maybe he was an old friend if the family or an uncle or something, judging by his grey hairs.'

'He's not old. A little silver at the temples: rather fascinating. As for a friend of the family's, he's a friend of my brother's, and he's also a friend of mine. So please don't run him down to me.'

'He looks the worst type of piker to me, but he's not my friend so what does it matter, and if he suits you you're welcome to him.'

'Thanks for giving me your permission,' I said.

'Oh gosh, Judy!' he wailed. 'Can't I say anything right?'

'You might try to.'

'You're a lovely girl,' he said bitterly. 'I come all this way to see you, and all you can do is pick on me. Let's get back to how it was before, Judy. How have things been with you? Tell me everything that has happened, and what your family are like, and all that.'

I began, reluctantly at first, to describe the family and odd little bits here and there. But I couldn't go far in any direction without stumbling against the dead girl in the garage. Everything seemed to come back to that in the end. Perhaps he'd appreciate Rex a little better then, as well as giving me a fresh angle on it all. So I gave it to him all, right from the beginning, just as I have written it down here. He listened in complete silence, but when I came to the bit where the sergeant let out that the girl was called Judith Allen, he pulled the car into the hedge, put on the brakes, and shut off the engine. He was silent for a long while when I had finished, scowling at the dashboard.

'This doesn't sound like a good business to me,' he said at last. 'Frankly, it sounds awfully deep and beastly. Don't you think so yourself?'

'Well, it was a beastly experience, if that's what you mean.'

'Not altogether,' he said seriously. 'It was just a coincidence, you think, that it happened to be you who found her, this girl who was using your name and was found dead in your garage the very day you came home?'

'Why — why, I don't know,' I stammered. 'I guess I haven't thought about it like that before. But I don't see — '

'Nor do I. But I certainly do wish you weren't all alone here.'

'Don't be silly, Bob,' I laughed. 'I'm not alone, there's all my family, and maybe Terence later, and — and — '

'Listen, Judy,' he faced around and took my hands in his. 'I'm not trying to *scare* you, see, but you want to be on your guard with these people,' he said earnestly. 'They may be your family, but you don't *know* them. Don't trust 'em, Judy, not any of 'em, not even your smart pal, Rex. Now don't get *mad* at me, Judy, I haven't said *anything* against them, I've only asked you to watch out. Don't take them at face value, that's all. It's common sense.'

'But you don't tell me what I've got to be careful of.'

'Because I don't rightly know, honey. Just be generally on your *guard*. Don't — don't sign any documents or — or anything of that sort. I wouldn't go wandering about the countryside alone at night, for instance. Oh, but common sense will tell you what to do, don't worry.'

I looked at him suspiciously. 'Do you think my family want to *murder* me? Nice ideas you have.'

'Now, Judy, I never suggested anything of the sort. I only want you to promise to be careful. Much as I dislike him, I believe that if you asked Mr. Brady outright about it he'd tell you the same.'

'Gee, it's a quarter to one already. We've got to beat it back to the house for lunch if we don't want to miss it altogether. All right, I promise.'

'Seal it with a kiss,' said Bob, landing one clumsily on the corner of my mouth. And before I had time to squawk at him, the car had let out a hungry roar and was eating up the road, its nose turned towards home.

⋆ ⋆ ⋆

Bob went back to town that evening. I was rather sorry to see him go; he could be so nice, like a brother, like I imagined Terry would be somehow.

I changed my dress and went downstairs. They were all in the little library, drinking cocktails before dinner. They were repeating to Neville what I had told them about the corpse in the car.

'I can tell you who she is now,' I chimed in. 'Our wonderful English police have tracked her down pretty smartly. She was an actress by the name of Averil Day. Ever heard of her?'

Neville put out his hand as if to clutch at Millicent's arm. His cocktail glass splintered noisily on the floor. 'God,' he said. 'Elsie,' and he keeled over.

Antonia half caught him as he fell, and braced herself against the weight of him. Together, we managed to push him down into an easy chair, and loosen his collar and tie. His head lolled greyly to one side. Millicent was wringing her hands and saying, 'Someone get some brandy or some sal volatile. Oughtn't you to make him put his head between his knees, Toni? Oh, lord, this is too — '

'For heaven's sake, Mother, stop flapping!' said Antonia sharply. 'Go and get the brandy yourself. Make yourself useful.'

Millicent distractedly teetered out of the room, muttering that it was too, too, terrible.

A tinge of colour crept back into the sallow skin, and the pale lashes fluttered slightly. Presently the greyish-blue eyes stared up at us fishily, uncomprehendingly.

He struggled to sit up. 'Did I pass out?'

'It's all right. Take it easy,' advised Toni.

'It's nothing really; dicky heart.' His eyes roved about the room. 'I think I'll be getting back now, if you don't mind.' He removed the cocktail I still grasped in my hand and drank it off. 'Thanks. I'm all right. I'd rather go now, before Milly comes back and starts fussing over me.' He stood up carefully.

'I'll come with you,' said Toni, cutting short his protest with, 'You look rotten. I'll take you home and leave you.' She stuck her head through the door. 'The coast's clear,' she announced.

They beat it a couple of minutes before Mother came back with an almost empty bottle. Then she saw there was no one in the room but me, and I had to explain to her that Neville had begged to be excused but had felt he wanted to get back home.

Millicent sat down. 'It's ghastly,' she said, clasping her temples in both hands. 'I don't understand it.'

'Understand what, Mother?'

'Poor man,' she said pitifully, 'what a shock!' Her face brightened suddenly. 'Judy, listen, I've a mind to try the crystal. Will you help me? Perhaps it will tell us something. Pull the curtains, dear, while I run upstairs and find the crystal.'

'What do you think it can tell us, Mother? Who Averil Day really was?'

Millicent shook her head. 'I know that,' she said. 'She was Elsie Thompson.

Neville's daughter!'

I said, 'But what on earth was she doing down here under — under my name?'

'Your name, child. What do you mean?'

I had forgotten for the moment that I had not told my family that the dead girl had been passing herself off as one, Judith Allen. I could have kicked myself now.

'She called herself Judith Allen,' I explained. 'Letters — and name-tabs on her clothes. Why?'

Millicent shivered. 'Baby!' she said. 'What did the police say?'

I shrugged. 'You know as much as they do.'

'I? Why do you say that? How should I?'

But before I could extricate myself, Toni came back, and we all three went in to dinner. I caught Millicent's warning look. The subject was not mentioned again that evening.

4

The Inquest

I didn't see poor Neville again till the day
of the inquest. It was held in an old tithe
barn. They told me inquests had been
held there from time immemorial, for
want of anywhere better. I was pretty well
the chief witness. Toni was rather nice to
me, seeing that I was nervous, and
Millicent wasn't much use, her nerves on
edge. Toni advised me what to wear and
that was how I found out she designed
stage-sets; otherwise I don't suppose she
would ever have told me. She seemed to
hate discussing her own affairs.

The tithe barn was striped patchily in
bright yellow sunlight and black velvet
shadow, and it took me some time before
I could see who was peopling the
dimness. There was a musty smell of hay
and grain that made me think of long
summer evenings when I was little, before

I went away. Babyface, the police constable I had met the day the poor girl died, came over out of the darkness and ushered me to a seat, unsmilingly, as though he had never seen me before; very intent on representing the majesty of the law. Toni, left alone, drifted into a seat elsewhere. She looked strangely excited, and her green eyes were glowing like a cat's in the darkness.

I saw Millicent come in, looking incredibly fair, with Neville. Remembering Neville's collapse that evening, I had expected to see him broken up, but he was the same as ever, except that his expression was suitably sober and he wore a discreet black tie. Babyface escorted them to the front row of benches.

The barn was filling up now, and there was a continuous rustling sound of whispering. Everyone stood up in a straggly fashion and sat down again. The coroner, a little man whose eyes were invisible behind his flashing pince-nez, sat down at his high desk at one end of the barn. Suddenly the desk appeared to be covered with a flurry of papers. The jurymen were being sworn. I felt nervous again, and automatically took out my compact and powdered my nose. I looked about fourteen in spite of my make-up, I thought disgustedly.

Someone called, 'Judith Allen!' and I stood up and walked forward. Babyface handed me a scruffy little puce-coloured book and gabbled without looking at me, 'You swear to tell the truth the whole truth and nothing but the truth so help you God?'

I said, 'Yes,' my voice a husky little whisper.

The story I told them was substantially the same as I have written here, except that the coroner was an impatient man and cut like a sword through any meandering. He was brusque, not unkind, but in somewhat of a hurry. I was glad when my turn was over.

They called Rex, who stood there looking very cool and handsome, answering their questions with calm assurance.

The sergeant gave evidence next. All reference to her masquerading as Judith Allen was kept well in the background, and if ever it raised its darkling head for a moment it was well and truly squashed by the ratty little coroner. The sergeant described how he traced the car to be a stolen one. Described how he had identified the dead girl as one Averil Day, an actress. Averil Day, he had subsequently discovered, was a stage-name, the deceased's real name was Elsie Thompson.

There was an undercurrent of rustling sound in the barn again, and I turned to look at the people whispering and staring covertly at Neville. I saw Rex's head bent towards a girl with a wing of copper hair glinting beneath the sweep of her hat. He was smiling at her. I felt a sort of angry pain in my chest and I wanted to do something showy to distract his attention from that awful girl, who looked horribly pretty from what I could see of her. I hated her..

When I next looked up, the police surgeon was on the stand rattling off technicalities which nobody understood. The jury fidgeted.

'The deceased must have absorbed at

least two drachms of paraldehyde,' averred the doctor.

'Would that be a sufficient quantity to kill her?' asked the coroner.

'Oh no. It can kill, if taken in large enough quantities, of course, but not this time, I think.'

'Then — ?'

'It is used as a hypnotic,' the doctor explained. 'Very powerful, and acts almost instantaneously.'

'How and when was this — er — drug taken, do you suppose?' asked the coroner.

'Can be taken subcutaneously with a hypodermic or orally. Found no hypodermic punctures on the skin, so presume it was administered orally. When? Wouldn't care to make a statement on oath on that point. Suggest it was administered *in the garage* — bear in mind that it acts immediately and she would have been quite unable to drive or even move after taking it — or else,' he hesitated and seemed reluctant to go on, 'it was taken earlier and *somebody drove the car with her in it into the garage.*'

It was very quiet for a few moments, and then there broke out an excited buzz of conversation. The coroner rapped angrily on his desk for order; and the noise subsided again.

'You mean,' said the coroner, 'that she was insensible *before* she came in contact with the carbon monoxide fumes?'

'Yes.'

'But death actually was caused by the noxious fumes and not by the drug. Am I correct?'

The doctor nodded.

There was some more jargon, and a revolting description of Elsie Thompson's lungs, which, he said, would have allowed him in the ordinary way to gauge roughly the time the paraldehyde was administered before death by the amount that had been dissipated by the lungs, unfortunately the carbon monoxide had made it impossible to judge anything with any certainty.

He stood down. And the coroner began directing the jury to their findings. If they believed the drug to have been self-administered they had still to consider whether the deceased had been a victim of misadventure or, being of a temporarily unbalanced mind, had in this manner taken her own life. On the other hand, if they believed the drug to have been administered by some person or persons unknown they had then to consider whether it was administered with malicious intent: their conclusions on this point would be largely affected by whether they decided that the drug had been taken in the garage or at some time previous.

I felt sick at the idea. The whispering was like leaves in a storm. Why should anyone want to kill that poor girl? Neville's daughter, I pondered, and she called herself Judith Allen? It was nonsense, yet suddenly I understood what Bob had meant when he said there was something beastly and incomprehensible about it.

The jury of nine men and three women filed slowly back to their places. The foreman stood there deprecatingly. 'We do not seem able to come to any agreement,' he said, and spread out his hands. 'The point has been accepted that if it had been suicide or misadventure there would have been some — some receptacle, a glass — '

'Quite, quite,' said the coroner dryly. 'Perhaps it is an 'open verdict,' that you require.'

The foreman bent over to discuss it with his colleagues. I pressed my hands together tightly between my knees, praying hard for an open verdict, without quite understanding why, just a kind of feeling that it would be a lot more comfortable if it was allowed to settle down quietly once more.

The foreman stood up again with an apologetic smile that seemed to say, 'Well, you know what women are, don't blame me.'

'We are unanimously agreed that the deceased died from carbon monoxide poisoning according to the evidence, by an act of some person or persons unknown of malice aforethought.'

My eyes moved round the barn, sliding over the familiar faces. Neville's drooping fishiness had resolved itself suddenly into cruel and bitter lines, he looked like an enemy, with his face carved out of iron. Beside him, Millicent seemed to have become smaller, and she looked frightened. Rex was watching me with alert guarded eyes; when he caught my glance he flashed me a smile. The girl beside him stood up, bored — the excitement was all over and one might as well go home, her pose seemed to say — or was I being ungenerous? Ah, and there was Toni at the back of the hall, smiling mysteriously, her eyes shining as if it was a particularly enjoyable party. I didn't think I could stomach any more. I asked Babyface appealingly if I might leave as I did not feel so good. He slid back the great wooden bolt that stretched right across the knotted oak door; and I slipped out gratefully into the sweet sunlight. Well, it was over anyway. I determined not to let death take possession of my thoughts.

Fortunately, the others seemed as reluctant to talk about it as I was. Conversation over dinner was not easy, the tide of it kept bumping us into that dangerous topic and then we'd eddy away from it nervously. I could not help asking Toni — a little bitterly — why she had looked so pleased and excited about it.

'Did I?' she said, stabbing a radish with her fork. 'As a matter of fact, I wasn't really paying attention to what was happening. The setting caught my imagination, it gave me an idea for a scene . . . that warm amber light streaking through the plum-bloomy shadows . . . and the way the faces loomed out a faint bluish-pink . . . and there was something about those heavy beams pressing down too. I want to put it down on paper — even a rough sketch — while I still have it clear in me.'

'Do you mean to say you were so absorbed in that that you didn't hear what they were saying? 'I said incredulously. 'Didn't you even hear the verdict? They said — Averil Day was murdered . . . '

'Did they?' Her face was sulky and absorbed.

'The toughest thing to me is that the poor kid had to die to make the front page,' remarked a strange male voice.

'Terry!' said Millicent, and her face lit up with an expression at once sad and beautiful. In that instant she had come alive, I realized, and she had not been really alive before.

I looked over my shoulder at the French windows wherein stood framed a young man of medium height with a kind expression; not so much handsome as good-looking, with his amber hair and eyes that looked light in contrast with his sun-tanned skin. He waved an evening paper in one hand. He came into the room without looking at me, and kissed Millicent. He ran his fingers lightly over the back of Toni's neck in passing, but she did not look up.

He bent over me, smiling.

'Before I kiss you, you *are* little sister, aren't you? I should hate to get slapped for my pains.'

I admitted I was; and he said, 'Welcome home, little sister,' in a way that made me feel he really was glad to see me again. My heart leapt out to meet his warmth and affection.

'Tell me everything, I want to hear it

all.' He pulled out a chair. 'I'm starving, Mother. Stay me with flagons and comfort me with apples.'

'Hullo, Terry,' said Toni suddenly, waking from her secret slumber. 'And what fetched you away from your nefarious doings this time?'

'Saw all these junketings with corpses going on in the old home,' he said, helping himself to cold sliced meat off the dish and deftly spearing chunks of salad, 'and rather thought you defenceless females might need a little . . . ' he paused for a word.

'Yah,' jeered Toni amicably, 'curiosity killed the cat and it might kill you! Watch out!'

He wrinkled his nose at her, his mouth too full for words. At length: 'So it was little sister who found Averil Day? Pretty tough on you, I must say. But, you know this, Averil — I had seen her in one or two shows, small parts, and I even met her once at a dull bohemian party. Not a bad kid; not talented, but ambitious and hard-working. Except for an extraordinary stroke of luck she would never have made the grade; that was why I felt it was so sad that she had to be murdered in order to get headlined.'

Toni looked at him oddly. 'Averil Day's real name was Elsie Thompson,' she said. 'She was Neville's daughter.'

'You don't mean it! That surely is the most amazing coincidence ever. Neville! Poor old devil! Is he very cut up about it?'

Millicent said faintly, 'Let us talk of something more pleasant, darling, do you mind?'

He flashed her a look of understanding. He began asking me about life in the States. We took coffee in the library, and afterwards Toni excused herself, because, she said, there was some work that she wanted to do — particularly. Terry was very entertaining. We were getting on well together, when he yawned, looked at his watch, and said, 'Ten o'clock. I think I'll go for a stroll before turning in. Good-night, Mother. Night, Sis. Bless you both. I shan't be late.'

I remembered that Toni had said there was a lady in the neighbourhood who was mainly responsible for Terry's appearances at home. I smiled and bet myself a dollar that that was where his stroll was leading. Millicent caught the tag-end of my smile.

'He's a darling, isn't he?' I said.

She looked pleased. 'I'm rather partial to him myself,' she said.

'I'd never have thought he was older than Toni.'

'He's thirty, and she's only twenty-five or six, but in ways he's a mere child, full of simple gaiety. And he's trusting like a child, too; although, Judy, he has not been unhurt by life. No, it has not been altogether easy for him. Life has not always been fair.'

She looked at me accusingly, as though it was my fault somehow. 'Toni, of course, is a very different cup of tea; she's hard. She knows what she wants and she goes all out to get it. Whether her fiancé realises it or whether he is the type that doesn't mind being managed . . . '

'Fiancé?' I echoed. 'I didn't know she was engaged. She never mentioned it. She doesn't even wear a ring, does she?'

'Oh, nowadays, Judy, it seems the younger generation do not wear rings or any of those odious symbols . . . '

'Is she — is she in love with him? Somehow she looks so untouched, so uninterested in men.'

'She would like you to think not,' said Millicent, a trifle grimly. 'But Toni can't hide things from me: she's mad about him.'

'Who is he?' I asked.

'No one of any importance — so far, anyway. A producer and playwright, I believe, very modern. Curdie Baxter is his name. People never had such ridiculous names in my day; they all sound like gangsters nowadays.'

Later that night when I was alone I leaned out of my window and thought what a curious family they were, with their secret lives that they guarded so jealously from one another, but in vain. There was Toni and her fiancé, and Terry and his mysterious local maiden, and Millicent and Neville, which seemed strange in all truth. And I suppose if I was really honest, there was me and — and

Rex. No, that was not being honest. He was practically a stranger, and anyway it was all on my side, so it didn't really count. Yet I was idiotically disappointed that he had made no attempt to see me today. But why should he? Probably he was justifiably annoyed with me for dragging him into such a nasty position. I felt very sad. I remembered how he had smiled at the girl with red hair, as I had seen him smile at me. The pale moonlight shivered before my eyes and the leaves sighed in the night breeze. I wished I was thirty and beautiful and very sure of myself. It seemed an awful long time to wait. I wondered what sort of woman Rex admired. I wondered . . . I wondered till I felt restless and too miserable for bed. The long fingers of moonlight beckoned and, flinging a jacket round my shoulders, I stole from the room.

It was peaceful and lovely out of doors, and after a while I gave myself up to the charm of solitude and the unusual colour and scent of the world at night. I wandered through the garden and over the stream that formed its southern boundary and across Big Field, on and on. It was heavenly.

I was walking down a dark alleyway of trees when it happened. There was a colossal, incredible, bursting sound, as though the end of the world had come. I stood immovable with fright. Then pebbles and twigs came showering down on me out of nowhere, and the echoes screamed and then reverberated into silence. I stood there for an eternity, blind and deaf. Then I saw something dark move against the deep liquid shadows.

I stirred suddenly and shouted, 'Help!'

I could hear footsteps moving fast, crunching on the ground; and I found that I was trembling. A man came running through the trees, a bar of moonlight silvered his hair — then his face; and I saw it was Neville.

He said, 'Judith! You! My God, are you all right?'

'What happened? 'I said.

'I thought you were a poacher. You're not hurt, are you? I'm terribly, terribly, sorry, my dear, if I scared you.'

I saw then that he had a gun in his hand.

'You shot at me,' I said furiously 'Are you mad? You might have killed me.'

'Oh, don't,' he said. 'It has been a shock for you, of course.'

'A shock! What on earth were you doing, shooting without warning?'

'There might have been an accident,' he agreed. 'But, after all, a poacher can hardly expect to be warned. I was only going to wing him. I'm awfully sorry, my dear.'

'Is that what you would have said to Mother if you had *killed* me?' I was trembling with anger. 'I came out for a peaceful stroll before bed, little thinking it might prove to be my last.'

'Well, you were lucky really to get off with nothing worse than a fright. I did warn you the other night that there were poachers about.'

'Was that meant to be a warning? I'm afraid I didn't take it in. I didn't understand that the estate had become a kind of free-for-all shooting-gallery.'

'You're upset, old lady; but you mustn't

be unreasonable.'

My fury died away as suddenly as it had arisen.

Neville smiled at me, his snag-tooth glinting sheepishly in the moonlight. 'Beddybyes and a hot drink for you, and tomorrow you'll be different again,' he said pacifically, leading me in the back way through the still house.

He snapped up the kitchen lights and began bustling about with an air of familiarity, pouring milk into a saucepan and stirring in brown granules from a tin marked 'CHOCACREME.' He whisked the pan from the stove and poured the steaming liquid into the cup from two feet high, so that it foamed creamily. He presented it to me, smiling.

'If you are wise, old lady, you'll forget about this little incident. Don't misunderstand me; it's the sort of thing that would only worry Millicent if you told her.'

'As it happens, I never intended to tell her. Thanks for the drink,' I said coldly, and turned to go.

Millicent stood there, vast and ethereal in a negligee of white georgette and lace.

She smiled at me whimsically.

'Secrets from Mama, already? Midnight expeditions with gentlemen! I hope you're not a naughty girl . . . No, no, no,' she laughed, holding up one hand. 'I don't want to know. A promise is a promise. Never betray a confidence, darling, even to your mother.'

'It's nothing of the kind. No promise about it. I don't know why *he's* making such a fuss about it,' I looked at Neville standing by the stove, like a servant in disgrace unjustly. 'The beginning and the end of it was that I went for a moonlight walk — by myself, and Neville thought I was a poacher and took a pot-shot at me. He didn't come within a mile of me, but it startled me and I got windy, and he very kindly came back with me and made me a hot drink so that I should sleep well. That's all there was to it.'

Millicent gathered in my words slowly. When she had collected them all she stood there in silence for a while, her eyes widening till they seemed like two great grey lakes of ice . . . then she turned, still wordlessly, and went away.

74

Neville said morosely, 'Well, after that little fiasco I might as well tootle off. Nightie-night, old girl.'

I bolted the door behind him and switched off the lights. I had no one to blame but myself. Bob had warned me not to walk the countryside at night. As I groped my way to bed, moonlight streaming into his empty room told me Terry had not yet returned.

5

Death is Not Sweet

I must have slept soundly, for I never heard Terry come in at all. It was a glorious day, and last night's troubles disappeared in the sunshine. I was first in the breakfast-room. Toni joined me presently, sauntering in through the French windows in a scarlet swim-suit and a green wrap, a rubber cap swinging from her finger.

'I'm ravenous,' she announced. She examined the contents of the silver dishes greedily. 'I wonder why being virtuous makes one so hungry? I was up at six, did an hour's work, and then went for a dip. It was lovely. No one else there: the sea, the earth, the sky were all mine.'

'You might have given me a shout, for all that. I'd forgotten the bathing here; it's at Little Limpington, isn't it? Is it good?'

Toni nodded, her mouth full of kidney.

'We'll go together next time,' she promised. 'Didn't like to wake you up, you were sleeping so peacefully.'

I can't bear being looked at when I'm asleep or talked about when I'm not there. But Toni looked so cute I couldn't feel very angry, with her green eyes sparkling between her thick lashes, and her hair in little damp curls all over her neat head.

I said mischievously, 'You're looking very pleased with yourself. What's happened? Curdie Baxter coming to see you?'

Toni spluttered into her coffee. 'You little devil,' she said, staring at me incredulously.

'I saw it in the crystal,' I answered her unspoken question; and she giggled appreciatively. 'But why did you hold out on me? I was bound to find out sooner or later, wasn't I?'

'Sufficient unto the day . . . However, this *is* the day. If you hang about enough you'll probably see him.'

'Meaning, you'd rather I didn't.'

'Oh, lord, no,' she sounded bored. 'I'm not the jealous type.'

'Tell me about him. What's he like?'

'Clark Gable, only he's trained his ears to lie down,' she smirked.

But that was a joke, because when Curdie Baxter turned up he looked like nothing but a little man with big horn-rimmed glasses and thin hair. I wondered what Toni saw in him and supposed he adored her, but it didn't seem to come out that way. He didn't pay much attention to her, or anyone else. He was quiet, as if he was holding himself in reserve. Toni interpreted his remarks to us, the hoi-polloi. Not that he was snobbish or conceited; it was just that he seemed remote. She showed him her latest sketches, and he was silent for a long time while she explained the significance of what looked to me like a lot of senseless lines and squiggles.

Evidently it meant something to him, for his face lit up and he patted her on the back and said, 'Toni, you're a gem!'

And Toni looked awfully bucked and said, 'Is that what you wanted?'

Curdie said, 'I didn't know it, my dear, but it is — exactly.'

He turned to me. 'You may not know it, but your sister is remarkably sensitive and gifted. If she'd been given a chance . . . '

'Oh, shut up, Curdie, you're speaking out of turn,' Toni interrupted crossly. 'Do you want to come bathing with us this afternoon, kid? We'd like to have you. Be ready at two-thirty, then.'

I took that as my dismissal and left them alone.

I went rummaging upstairs in the boxroom, looking for my bathing-kit. Voices drifted up to me from the room beneath, distorted out of recognition. I found the things I was looking for, and slammed shut the trunk again. I opened the cupboard where the smaller trunks and cases were kept, out of harm's way, and began heaving them back inside. For some reason the sound came up more clearly in there. I heard Neville's unmistakable voice say, 'She's a nice little girl, a plucky little girl, isn't she? I don't think she has any idea at all of what she is up against.'

And my mother's voice, reedy and

frozen as an icicle, 'What *is* she up against, Neville? I'm afraid I'm as ignorant as she is. I should have said she was very fortunate, on the contrary; she's got everything.'

'Yes, hasn't she, poor little rat?' said Neville. 'Someone ought to explain things to her. She ought to be warned . . . '

Mother said, 'Of what do you think she ought to be warned? Eh?'

There was a silence, and all I could hear was my heart beating.

And then Neville said almost dreamily, 'It was curious that fortuitous resemblance between your child — and mine, Milly, wasn't it? There can't have been many people who knew about it — yet someone tried to take advantage of it. Cruel, cruel, when they were both so young. But it was my child, Milly, that was killed. Poor little Elsie!'

'Stop play-acting, Neville. What is it you want?'

'Oh, my dear, my dear, you're very heartless, very cold to me now. It used not to be so. What balm *can* there be for a father's broken heart? How would you feel if it was *your* daughter? I want to spare you that pain, I want to save her.'

'This is sheer gibberish. What do you want? Tell me what you want plainly. I don't trust you, Neville, when you're in this sort of mood.'

'I can see that. If I seem any different it's because I'm suffering. But you wouldn't understand that, my dear. You're tired of me, aren't you? And a little afraid, I think. It occurred to me that you might prefer me to leave your employment. It might be easier if I went away. I could go, if it was worth my while . . . '

'I see,' said my mother in a small cold breath. 'So that is the tune you want me to dance to. You never did love me. I know that now. Part of an elaborate game with your own god, wasn't it? And now that my husband has died and altered the situation, you too have swung over on to the other side, in order to be near your god.'

Neville chuckled. 'I'm very fond of you, Milly. Make no mistake about that. But surely a fellow-feeling should make us wondrous kin. For we worship the same

81

little god, don't we, my snow-maiden?'

'You must think me a fool,' she said contemptuously. 'You don't know me. I'll never submit to *blackmail*.'

'Blackmail!' Neville's voice was suddenly terrifyingly venomous. 'If you want to use hard names for things, there are one or two *I* can use. I answer your word 'blackmail' with the word MURDER — '

But I could bear no more, not another word. I banged to the cupboard door and leant against it, shaking. There was a taste of blood in my mouth from where I had bitten my hand savagely to keep from crying out. After what seemed a long while, I picked up my things and went downstairs.

I thought luncheon would be unendurable, but it passed quite pleasantly, after all. Terry was there and very gay. I listened to the laughter and talk floating around me and wondered whether perhaps I had dreamt it all.

I felt defenceless, having no one to turn to, no one to trust. If only Rex . . . But he was a stranger, and besides, he wasn't interested. I wondered if I dared write to

Bob. Somehow I didn't want to put anything down on paper — there wasn't really anything precise enough to put down, when I came to analyse it. I'd have to drag the load around with me a little while longer, that's all.

Toni drove Curdie and I down to the sea afterwards. Little Limpington was a hamlet on the coast that had not changed in a hundred years. We drove slowly along the sea-road in search of a suitable bathing spot. There was no beach, the sea came up high against the cliff which was covered with a coarse grass and clumps of thrift and sea-pink bringing up the colour, here and there.

We flung ourselves down in the deep grass and stared up at the patched blue sky that seemed a long way up in the bluest places. There was a wind, but the sun was warm. Toni stood up, slim and scarlet against the blue, like a poster.

'Who's coming?' she said. 'You're not going to stew there, are you?'

'Later,' I promised drowsily. 'I want to get thoroughly baked.'

Toni walked beyond my vision. There

was silence, then a splash, and silence again.

I made my mind a blank. In a little while Curdie rolled over and began talking to me about Toni and her talent that almost amounted to genius. He explained to me that the funny little incomplete sketch she had shown us earlier was a kind of notation for a dramatic version he was making of Crime and Punishment. He talked as if I must know all about Crime and Punishment, whatever it was, and I didn't like to interrupt him. It seemed to be very dreary, anyhow, as he explained it, all about a young man who kills an old woman with an axe and then spends the rest of his time trying to make up his mind whether he is sorry or not. Only it wasn't easy, he said, to translate it into the medium of the theatre. And that was just where Toni was so marvellous. In some extraordinary way she was able to convey the whole atmosphere of a scene in a few strokes of colour, while it was still hanging wordlessly in his head. He saw it all clearly now, thanks to her.

Of course, even if anyone could be found to back it, it couldn't possibly be a success, he quite realized that. But he had plans. If only he had money — or a really sound backer who had complete confidence in him and cared more about art than profit-making.

He took off his glasses and polished them. Without them he looked boyish and excited. His great ambition was to have a theatre of his own, he'd call it the English Theatre, and it would be something representative and yet new. He'd put on good, sound stuff in an exciting way, so that it really meant something, really moved people; and then, oh, very occasionally, he would put on a new piece by anyone, he didn't care who, so long as they had something to say and a new way to say it. His theatre would come to mean *the* theatre.

His enthusiasm was infectious. And though he was dull enough away from his pet subject, he had made me see his little-boy charm and where his attraction lay for Toni. I had no doubt of his ability, or that he would somehow succeed.

'Well, I'm going in now,' he said abruptly. He folded his spectacles carefully, placed them on his towel, and stood up, wiry and slender.

Listening to him had chased my miseries away, and I went down with him to the water. The grass was rough and prickly to my bare feet. Curdie went in first in a bad dive that was too shallow. I stood on the edge pulling on my bathing-cap and watching the water, a few inches below, bounced by the wind into tiny waves.

Toni's voice blew back to me faintly, 'About time too. I was just coming out.'

I filled my lungs, swung my arms up and out, and dived.

I came up and looked around. The water was cold and invigorating after my sun-bath. Toni was treading water, talking to Curdie. I went under again and swam deep till I saw her legs like pale stalks waving. I grabbed at them and pulled her down, grinning into her startled face. We came to the surface, spluttering. We played water-tag, the three of us, till Toni said sharply, 'Curdie, you're cold. Go in.'

He certainly was a curious pale blue. He turned obediently and began making for shore, with Toni swimming slowly behind him. I watched them heave their bodies out of the water, past the white chalk space, and on to the grass. I waved, turned, and began swimming away out to sea.

I swam steadily, with long slow strokes towards the horizon. The purifying salt water washed my distress away. I didn't just shut my mind to it, it really cleansed it right off so that it didn't matter anymore and it might as well never have been. When I had swum far enough I turned back. I could see the curving white arms of the little bay beckoning to me in welcome. It looked very peaceful and sweet.

I must have swum out about a mile and I was pleasantly tired when I made my way into the semi-circle of the bay again. For an instant I thought I had somehow mistaken the bay and swum back to a different one. It didn't look the same. I paddled gently up and down, frowning. Then I saw what it was, and I thought my heart would stop.

The cliff had suddenly grown much higher. There was quite an expanse of white chalk now between the grey sea and the tufted green grass at the top. It didn't make sense at first: a nonsensical bit of magic. But a cold worm of fear at the pit of my stomach told me what it was. *I had forgotten the tide*. And the tide was going *out!*

I swam towards it slowly. When I was close enough, I threw myself out of the water as high as I could. My fingers tipped the drooping blades of grass before I fell back. I tried again, clutching a clump of thrift which came away in my hand. I floated away from the side and called: 'Toni . . . Cur-die . . . Toni!' as loudly as I could. The sound flew up into the sky and back again with a small metallic echo. I went back to the cliff-face and tried again. I kept on trying till my fingers caught firm hold and dug themselves deeply into the earth. But the muscles in my arms were too tired to obey my orders; they could not pull up my body which the sea encircled in a clinging embrace. I slipped back and the water closed over my head. I wondered whether I could possibly keep afloat till the tide went right down; and I went down a long way to find the bottom. But I knew it was hopeless, already the strain was beginning to tell. I floated on my back again, calling from time to time, but my voice sounded so frightened on the empty air that presently I stopped. Besides, it was no use staying afloat when the chill eating into my bones now counteracted the little rest it gave me, and my eyes painfully watched the water subsiding inch by inch. Was there no foothold anywhere? I scanned the cliff-face for the millionth time.

A darkness on the shadowed side of the bay caught my attention. A little way down from the top a piece jutted out — it was less than a ledge — and precariously a tamarisk had rooted itself there, spilling its brave pink fronds downwards. I swam to it eagerly, flinging myself upward, clutching at its overhanging branches as if it were hope itself. If only it held! I clung to it desperately, panting, my body half out of the water, clasping my waist with its wet chill fingers, pulling me back, pulling me down, dragging me back to its deathly bosom. I — would — not — let — go. Somehow I contrived to loosen its drag, got free, my knees grazing on the stubborn chalk, till my feet gripped it too. I stuck there, like a fly on a wall, hanging on the tamarisk shrub, and listening to the water slapping crossly at my heels, 'Come back! Come back!' I edged very slowly up the cliff, tugging at the shrub. There cannot have been much earth on that jutting piece of chalk that was too small to be called a ledge. The little tree shuddered beneath my weight. There was a tearing sound and little lumps of chalk struck me sharply as I hurtled backwards, bearing with me a jumbled vision of pink tamarisk and jagged clouds and water.

The water said, 'There!' triumphantly, and pushed me down and down, poking its cold grey fingers in my ears and eyes and nose, choking my lungs with its beastliness. I fought my way to the surface again; not with courage now but from sheer panic — fighting, unreasonable panic. I knew my last chance had gone. I knew I could never make the cliff-top now: the water was too low, and I was too exhausted. I was going to drown. I — Judith Allen — was going to *drown*. Black fear rode me: I shouted madly and struggled with the water.

Then another sound penetrated the noise I was making. Someone was hallooing me furiously. It took a long while for my muzzy consciousness to realize that it was Rex, standing on the cliff-top calling to me. When he saw that he had attracted my attention he lay down on the grass with his head, shoulders and arms hanging over the edge, for me to grip. But it was useless. I was too tired. I could never make my way across to him now. I could feel my body slipping downward through the water. It wasn't cold any more, it was velvet-smooth and dark . . .

'Ju-dith! Ju-dith!' The sound, relentless and persistent, gave me no peace; it was harsh and compelling. It compelled me, urged me, forced me across the narrow strip of water to where he lay, insisting that I obey him. With a last tremendous effort I lifted my leaden arms, and he caught my cold wrists in his strong warm hands.

'Easy does it, easy, Judy,' he said softly. He edged backwards inch by inch, taking the weight of me on his wrists and elbows. I seemed to hang there for an eternity. As he drew me level, I could see his white teeth bared in a grin of pain, and drops of sweat running down from his temples and shining on his cheeks. His breath came in little grunts. One more huge pull, and he tumbled back, with me on top of him, on to the good, safe earth.

He put his arms about me and I lay there, still as the dead, letting the sun warm me back to life and the steady thud of his heart beneath mine reassure me, comfort me. He stroked my wet hair gently.

Pretty soon I began to feel better and sat up. I stared at my hands still puckered from immersion and faintly blue.

I laughed, and pushed my hair off my forehead. I guessed I looked an awful fright with all the make-up washed away and my hair a dank, wet tangle. Rex certainly managed always to see me at my worst: I could hardly have any glamour for him in the circumstances.

'What happened?' said Rex gently.

I told him how we all three had gone bathing and they had left the water first, and I had gone for a long swim and found, on my return, that the tide was going out — and I had forgotten all about the tides.

'Didn't either of them mention it to you?'

I shook my head.

'Well, where are they, anyway? Did they just walk out on you or did they tell you they were going?'

'I called . . . and they were gone.'

'It's incredible,' there was restrained anger in his voice. 'Wait a minute.' He stood up and strode over to where my bathing things still lay in a meek little heap, waiting. He brought them across to me. 'They did leave you a note,' he said grudgingly. 'Pinned on top of your things.'

'Read it to me,' I said, tugging a comb through the wild mess of my hair. My only concern just then was to make myself look like a human being once again.

He read, 'Gone to look for Eskimo pies. Back in ten minutes.' He frowned at me.

'Ices,' I interpreted. 'They've gone to look for ice-cream. And as for 'back in ten minutes,' that's a figure of speech, you know.'

'I'll say it is.' He looked grim. He held out his hands to me. 'I'm going to take you home, my dear, while you're still in one piece. Do you think you can walk to the car, or shall I carry you?'

He tucked the lap-rug snugly round me. And I lay back limply, watching his stern profile as he drove.

'Words are very inadequate,' I said presently. 'How can I thank you properly for saving my life?'

He took his hand off the wheel and patted mine. 'I don't want thanks, my dear. I only thank God that I was in time.'

'Even so — your resourcefulness — I

should be dead now, that's all I know,' I said, and shuddered.

'Oh, my dear, don't,' he said, and stopped the car. His face was close to mine. And then his lips pressed down fiercely, blotting out the sun, and I was drowning again, but this time I was drowning in sweetness and bliss . . .

I laughed shakily. 'How you can kiss me when I look such a sketch!'

'Little darling, little love,' he murmured. 'I nearly lost you.' His face was screwed up. 'It makes me feel ill even to think of it. You must take great, great care of yourself. Promise me. Please! For my sake.'

'I didn't do it on purpose, you know.'

'You're such a guileless little thing.'

'You make me sound half-witted. It was a thing that might have happened to anyone.'

'Oh that, yes.' His hand stroked my arm gently. 'You're so trusting, Judy. You're nothing but a child, and you don't understand what you're up against. How should you?'

'Why, that was what Neville said,' I

cried, before I had time to think. 'What am I up against?'

But he made me tell him first what Neville had said. And that led somehow to my midnight walk the night before and how Neville nearly shot me, thinking I was a poacher. Rex listened to it seriously, holding me close against him, as if I might escape even now. But when I had finished, he refused to tell me what he believed me to be up against.

'No,' he said tenderly. 'You've had quite enough horrors for one day. Home, now. And we'll talk of this again, I promise; because it is important. And till I see you again you've just got to take care of your precious little person.'

He kissed me again. 'I wouldn't make too much of your misadventure,' he warned me. 'Take it casually if you have to mention it at all. Someone might be interested in it, I fear. Be on your guard, and keep among people all you can.'

I crept into the house and up to my room without being seen by anyone. I lay on my bed, thinking, and watching the sun slip across the ceiling. I heard a car drive up, the doors slamming, and then Toni running lightly up the stairs, calling my name.

I yoo-hooed back.

She came in and stood looking down on me.

'Well, what in the world happened to you?' She sounded annoyed.

I blinked up at her. 'Rex Brady picked me up in his car and drove me back. There didn't seem much point in waiting for you any longer. I wasn't even sure you meant to come back: you'd been gone a long time.'

'I left a note for you that I was coming back. Did you think I'd forget about you or leave you stranded miles from anywhere? You might at least have had the forethought to leave a message for us in return before dashing off into the blue with your boyfriend.'

'Honestly, I didn't think you were coming back. I didn't know it took such a time to get ices in this country.'

'They didn't have any at Little Limpington. We went to Sarset; early closing. We went on to Arnley; they were sold out. We seemed fated. And I was determined to get those damned ices, cost what it might . . . We *did* get them, and you can imagine we felt pretty narked when we trailed all the way back with them and then found our bird had flown. And then I wondered what on earth had happened to you and was flapping round in circles, when Curdie made me drive back and see if you'd arrived, before I tottered grey-haired to an early grave.' She laughed. And I laughed politely with her. 'All the same, Judy, do be more considerate and leave a message another time.'

I raised my eyebrows. 'I guess we're quits this time.' I yawned and rolled over on my side. 'Think I'll take a little nap before dinner,' I said.

The door banged behind her.

I felt fine once more when I awoke. I looked at myself curiously in the mirror as I made up my face. Was I pretty? Hair curling softly under in a golden page-boy, brushed away from a round forehead. Blue eyes. I wished my nose wasn't so snub. You can't look really grown-up with a snub-nose. A curly pink mouth, yes, even I could see my mouth was pretty nice. And a little round chin to finish off my round face. My figure was all right, thank goodness, a good torso and a flat waist and hips that tapered off into long well-shaped legs, tanned and slim. When I looked at myself in the glass it meant Judith Allen to me, but what, I wondered, did it mean to other people. What, for instance, did it mean to Rex? He kissed me and said some nice things, but was he saying them to *me?* In books one always knew these things at once. I had supposed one did in real life too. When Rex kissed me it made me feel different from anything I have ever known; and yet — and yet I didn't feel sure and confident about him the way I did about Bob. Perhaps that was because I was in love with him and it blurred my vision, whereas Bob was just a brother to me.

I ran the lipstick over my mouth, took one last glance at myself in the mirror, and went downstairs.

6

I Find Out What I'm Up Against

Terry leant across the dinner-table. 'Livvy's throwing a little 'do' tonight and she wants us all to go. You and Curdie aren't doing anything particularly wild, are you, Toni?'

'Very civil of Miss Fane to ask us, I'm shaw,' said Toni primly. 'Me young man and me ull be ever so pleased.'

'And Judy, of course. Got anything in long pants you'd like to bring with you, Sis?'

Toni chanted, 'Beau Brummell Brady can fetch her away, on a cold and frosty morning!'

I coloured up. 'I don't suppose he'd want to come,' I said defensively. Then Terry chimed in:

'Certainly he'll come! Though I must confess, sweetheart, that I am disappointed in your taste. I had pictured some husky Texan, yearning beneath a yellow moon to the rhythm of a hill-billy.'

'I thought Rex was a friend of yours,' I said crossly.

'Oh, well, I'm a funny lad and I have a lot of funny friends, that's nothing to go by,' he smiled at me winningly.

'He also happens to have saved — to have got me out of some sticky places . . . Very kind, he's been,' I stammered hotly.

I saw Toni kick Terry under the table before he had time to answer. He cut back his retort and turned to Millicent to ask her if she was coming with them.

Millicent raised her head dreamily from the astrology paper she was studying.

'No, children, I won't come out, thank you very much. I don't feel in the mood, and I think Neville would be glad. The police are being so tiresome, and they keep pestering the poor fellow with all manner of idiotic questions. It is really most inconsiderate of them. However, we don't want to think about these unpleasant things, do we? Are you all taking care of Judith and seeing that she has plenty of fun and thrills?'

So we left Millicent behind with horoscopes and astrological prophecies and Neville for company. On our way across we stopped at Rex's bungalow; but he was out. Olivia Fane lived in one of those cunningly reconstructed cottages where all the 'olde worlde' charm has been retained and every modern convenience added.

Olivia Fane's home had a genuinely good feeling when you stepped in. This was all right, you felt. Miss Fane came over to us, copper hair piled high on her small head, wearing a dull bronze taffeta housegown that rustled a tarnished green. She looked like one of those incredible photographs in *Harper's Bazaar*; she had that same, almost subdued, glittering, beauty. I realized, too, that she was the girl Rex had sat next to at the inquest — only she wasn't a girl, she was about thirty-five. Not that she looked old, she looked ageless; and I could believe she bowled men over.

She made me feel an awful frumpish gawk, though she didn't mean to. A mean streak in me was glad Rex was not there to see us side by side. Of course Rex was more suitable for her in a way than Terry, because he was around her age,

There were one or two other people there when we arrived; dull, horsey-faced creatures of no importance. Olivia was very sweet, and managed to make you feel at home. Later, she showed me over the house. And she was one of the few people I've ever met who didn't ask you a lot of silly questions as though you were a kid still at school.

Her bedroom was pretty terrific, like something in a film. And she showed me her glass wardrobe that lit up with electric light inside when it was opened. I never have seen so many clothes outside a shop.

But she explained to me then that she was the editress of *Chic*, the world-famous fashion paper, and one simply had to dress up to it. Besides, clothes were one of the perks of the job

It must be very thrilling, I said. She laughed, and said one got used to it, and hadn't we better go down and find the others.

I sat on a pouffe, nursing my drink, and

watched her with Terry and the other men, wondering which of them she liked the best. Then I came to the conclusion that none of them meant anything, she was so aloof and cool. Her face never lit up or changed its faintly smiling expression.

I wondered if I could ever be like that. I determined to take her as my model. Though how I was ever to fix my hair that way was more than I would know. Maybe when I knew her better I could ask her to advise me..

'Enjoying yourself, funny-face?' asked Terry some time later. And, 'How do you like Livvy?'

'Gosh, Terry, she's wonderful, isn't she!'

'Thattaway, is it?' he laughed. 'I'll tell her how you feel about it; she'll be flattered.'

But I made him swear not to be such a cad.

He laughed again. 'Livvy's not like that. She just happens to have been born beautiful and her job happens to be dress, and there's nothing more miraculous about her than that.'

'Glamour,' I said. 'You can't fake that. Is she going to marry you, Terry?'

'We-el,' he said, opening his amber eyes very wide, 'I'll let you know when I've asked her.'

'I didn't mean to be nosy. Only, you must be awfully in love with her.'

'All right, all right. You're too young to know about such things, Judy.'

Mother's light was out when we reached home. I went to bed, and when I did drop off eventually it was to dream I was back in the bay, drowning. I woke up with it once or twice, and once I thought I heard the Elder Hall ghost, but I guess I was a bit jumpy.

Curdie went back to town after breakfast. Toni drove him to the station. I went in to see Millicent. She was at her spindle-legged escritoire, almost smothered in papers and documents.

'Oh, my God,' she groaned when she saw me. 'Don't come near me, I'm practically demented. Anyone would think I had *never* paid a bill. I don't know where they all come from, I'm sure. I think they just keep on sending in the same old bills time after time, even though they've been paid.'

'But they can't do that, Mother, they're all properly receipted, aren't they? You keep them all, don't you?'

'Don't ask me, pet. They must be somewhere about, but where? Here are all these damn papers to do with the estate, but how on earth am I to check up on them, I ask you? Neville never makes out a proper statement. I'm a fool to trust him, aren't I?' She leant back and ran her fingers through her silvery locks. 'What do I know about him, after all? He's practically a complete stranger . . . The fact is, I met him somewhere or other — an Old Harringovian, down on his luck, and all that sort of thing — and I took pity on him. I needed a bailiff at the time, for Simpson was no earthly good . . . Yes, I know your father swore he was a wonder, but the fact remains he never did a stroke of work after your father went to America. So I took on Neville . . . Perhaps I should never have let him become so friendly . . . It's a mistake to become too intimate with one's employees — but I thought he was a gentleman, Judy . . . I'm not so sure now. You know, Terry says he robs me right and left. He probably does; but what can I do without proof?'

'How can he rob you?' I asked curiously.

'Well, I don't really understand it myself. I'm a fool about money and things like that. The sort of thing I believe happens is that he'll sell the apple-crop in the spring on its blossom; the whole orchardful for so much down, regardless of whether frost or disease ruins the lot. It saves a lot of trouble and risk; on the other hand, you don't get anything like as much money for your crops. He sells it outright, and then when the season comes, before the dealer comes to strip the trees, he goes round and carefully removes half the fruit and sells it locally by the pound, and pockets the money. Pretty!'

'But, Mother, that's dishonest,' I gasped. 'You can't let him do that.'

'I know,' said Millicent uneasily. 'But I

don't actually *know* if it's true.'

'Well, you ought to ask him. Do *something*,' I said sternly.

'I know,' she said again. 'I'm desperately worried about it all, baby. All this responsibility for a woman alone . . . A place like this *eats* money. I don't know where it goes . . . I never spend a penny on myself. Of course the children's education . . . '

She flung her pen down in disgust. 'Bah! If I could afford it I'd have a secretary. I honestly believe it would pay me in the long run . . . Poor child, I'm making you as depressed as myself. It's too bad . . . '

'I feel most awfully helpless. I wish there was something I could do.'

She looked at me speculatively. Then she shook her head, smiled, and patted my cheek gently. 'Bless you, darling. It'll all come right with a little perseverance. I never should have told you about it but for my crazy habit of thinking aloud. You run along now and leave your silly old mother to worry it out by herself.'

Obediently, I ran away. It was time to

make ready for my date with Rex. And I didn't want to miss that.

I could see Rex's panama bobbing along beneath the trees. I called, and he turned and flourished his stick at me, waiting for me to catch up with him.

'Hullo,' he said. 'Fit enough for a good walk?'

'Sure,' I said sturdily, without looking at him. Truth to tell, I was disappointed at his casual greeting. I had hoped he would kiss me. Maybe yesterday had just been an accident, after all, and didn't mean a thing. I sighed.

He turned. 'What's the matter? Am I walking too fast for you?'

'Oh, I'm so miserable! I loathe this beastly, mad world, where everything goes wrong.'

'Ah ha, and what did you have to drink at the fair Olivia's party? I diagnose this as a hangover.'

'How did you know about Olivia's party? We called for you and you were out.'

'Was I, now! Ah well, I keep my ear to the ground, you know.' He laughed and pinched my arm. And then somehow I felt better.

At the top of the hill was a clump of beech trees, and we lay on the grass beneath their shade. The sky was cloudless. High up an unseen lark was singing. Rex took my chin in his hand. 'Aren't I going to get my good-morning kiss?'

But I suddenly felt shy. 'No,' I said.

He caught me by the shoulders, pulled me forward and kissed me roughly on the mouth.

My hand seemed to come up of its own accord and hit his cheek smartly.

There were tears in my eyes. I pulled away from his grasp and ran down the hill, stumbling, unable to see for the tears . . . I hated him . . . Never wanted to see him again . . . Wanted to die . . . He'd made me look a fool . . . I could hear his steps padding behind me as I ran. He caught up with me and swung me round into his arms, holding me tightly and kissing me, without speaking. When I opened my eyes he was looking down at me seriously, questioningly. But still he said nothing, only began gently kissing the tears off my face and stroking my hair. When he touched me I felt as though moths were fluttering inside me, and I wanted badly to kiss him back wildly and to stay close in his arms for ever and ever. But I felt too shy, and I just stood there, waiting.

'You're very sweet, little Judy,' he said at last. 'Forgive me for making you cry. I'm only a stupid brute. But I was thinking of your good name. You can have no idea how much I wanted to take you in my arms when I turned round and saw you this morning, so fresh and beautiful. But someone might have been watching, so I didn't. And I couldn't look at you all the way up. And then I was clumsy and annoyed you: you were quite right to slap my face. Only, you should have done it harder. Do it again.' He thrust his jaw forward invitingly.

'Oh, Rex,' I said.

He smiled at me whimsically. 'I ought to have more restraint, at my age. But, you see, you're so very lovable, darling; you just make a man's heart go to water

. . . Judy, may I ask you a question?'

I said, 'Yes,' breathlessly.

'Are you in love with that young American who turned up the other day?'

'Bob?' I laughed. 'Good heavens, no.'

He smiled. 'Are you in love with *anyone*?'

I looked away at the blue curve of trees on the horizon. 'Yes . . . '

I heard him say, 'Then, of course you'd rather I didn't kiss you . . . Well,' in a very dry, business-like voice, 'we'd better get on with our little talk. Shall we sit down and make ourselves comfortable?'

I felt very unhappy at the way he had misunderstood, but I hadn't the face to explain to him. We sat down with our backs against the rough bark of an oak.

He said, 'This is not a thing for you to be frightened about. It's possible, you see — I won't say anything more definite than that — but it is possible that someone is trying to — what's that Americanism? — to rub you out.'

'Why, who on earth would want to, Rex? You're joking!'

'I'm not. I don't know *who* it would be;

112

it might be almost anyone among the people around you today. It doesn't seem reasonable to suppose that all the funny things that have happened since you arrived have been mere coincidental accidents, does it?'

'I hadn't thought about it.'

'Listen, Judy, did you never ask yourself *why* this Elsie Thompson or Averil Day should be murdered?'

'Well, how should I know? She was a stranger, and goodness knows what she was up to in her private life.'

'Ah, but you and I know something more than the rest of them know, don't we? We know that she was pretending to be Judith Allen. She had her own ideas about that, I expect. But supposing that someone thought she was the real Judith Allen; what then? They wanted to get rid of Judith Allen for some reason — so they somehow induced her to take this paraldehyde stuff and left her there insensible with the engine running . . . '

'It could have been an accident,' I said stubbornly.

'The coroner thought not. Anyway, it

can't have been an accident that she was passing herself off as you. She must have seen a photo of you somewhere, for she had made herself look as much like you as possible. Same style of dress, hair, and everything. She wasn't like you at all really, and yet in the garage that day I noticed the resemblance at once. And then, mark you, she was not just any actress, but Neville Thompson's daughter. And Thompson, you will remember, took a shot at you the other night. On a bright moonlight night he mistook you for a poacher, long fair hair and all.'

'I was behind the trees,' I protested. 'He can't have seen me very plainly. Besides, he had mentioned about the poachers some days before.'

'You don't know what direction the shot came from, you only know that when at last he came to you he came through the trees. And of course he mentioned the fact that the poachers were getting very bad; therein lies the whole point of his story.'

'But he'd never kill his own daughter, Rex.'

'I'm not adding up this sum, my dear, I'm merely writing down the figures for you as they come. The next item is yesterday's little trouble — which so very nearly succeeded, only I happened to come along and spoil it. It was bad luck from the murderer's point of view, because it might have been a week before anyone else chanced to pass that way. You'd have been washed up miles farther along the coast by then. That was a clever plan, so simple, so ingenious; it could never seem anything but an accident.'

'Neville wasn't there. I don't see how he could possibly have had anything to do with it,' I said slowly.

'No,' he agreed, 'not this time.' His dark face was solemn. 'Only Antonia — or Curdie — or perhaps both.'

The sun pulled a cloud in front of its face. I felt very cold and alone. Presently, Rex took one of my cold hands gently in his.

'But not my own sister,' I whispered incredulously.

'Baxter is a very ambitious young man. He wants money — badly. I think he'd do anything for money so that he can have this silly theatre he's so crazy on. You can tell the theatre means more to him than any person, more even than Antonia. And Antonia hasn't any money of her own, so they can't get married, yet. She'd marry him and live in a garret like a shot, if he asked her. But he won't ask her for fear of spoiling his chances elsewhere. And mind you, she's ambitious for him. She worships him, Judy. It's my belief she'd do anything for him.'

'Murder?'

'That is a harsh word. All she had to do was *not* warn you of the tide, and then go riding away for an hour or so till it was all over.'

'I can't *believe* it, Rex. Why *should* anyone want to murder me?'

'Dear, you're an heiress now. That's the beginning and the end of it. Your father left all his money to you, didn't he?'

I nodded. 'Mother gets the estate. I don't know why he did it that way. I knew nothing about it, anyway, till the old lawyer told me afterwards ... But if that's the way Dad wanted it — '

116

'The others get nothing, you see, and your mother practically nothing. He was their father as much as yours, they had a right to expect — '

'I don't see they had any right. He must have had some reason for acting that way, he was always the wisest, most just man that ever lived. And he gave Mother a pretty whopping allowance during his lifetime too.'

'Judy, don't think I'm making excuses for them, I'm only trying to make it all clear to you . . . Here is your mother at fifty, suddenly left almost penniless — penniless from her standpoint, that is. It's no joke, particularly when you are of a careless, extravagant nature, as I guess your mother to be. And then I think she is rather influenced by Neville, whom I judge to be a pretty bad hat, and he may have made some unequivocal suggestions. I don't say he has, mind, or that she would listen if he did. I know I'm putting all manner of horrible ideas in your head; but don't jump to conclusions, for all that. This will of your father's, now. Who inherits after you? The money's in trust for you at present, isn't it?'

'Yes. I don't get control of it until I'm twenty-one. I can use the interest, but not the capital, or even will it away, until I attain my majority. Unless I happen to marry before then, then it is handed over to me. But if I die before then, Mother gets the interest during her lifetime and the capital is held in trust for Terry and Toni until she dies. I think that is how it works . . . ' I hesitated. 'You don't really think they want to — to get rid of me for my money, Rex? Why, if they asked me, I'd give them whatever they wanted. I don't need all that amount. I do wish now that Father had never done it. It's rotten somehow — a kind of mean temptation. But even so, I can see how it would work out for Mother; but the others, what benefit would they get?'

Rex said. 'You are getting the low-down on everything, aren't you? I'm sorry. Neville is more than a bailiff, more than a friend to your mother, my child. Now that your father is dead, there is no reason why they should not marry. Very convenient for Major Thompson. Millicent is a generous woman. As for your sister or her young man, once you are out of the way, she can borrow up to the hilt on her expectations. Or if she was quite innocent of the intrigue and Curdie arranged it by himself, he would then marry her and use his husbandly coercions to persuade her, to borrow on her future inheritance. It has been done before now.'

I felt sick. 'I wish to God I'd stayed in the States.'

'Poor child, I expect you do. But it is possible, I'm afraid, to hire people.'

It seemed to me that the world had shrunk to the size of a marble and there was nowhere on it where I could hide. Was this what money did to you? But you couldn't kill a person unless you hated them, however much you wanted money. And what harm had I ever done to any of these people — so how could they hate me?

'What am I to do, Rex?'

'Be on your guard, my dear, be careful . . . This chap,' he added thoughtfully, 'that you're in love with. Can't he do something?'

'Why, what on earth could he do?'

'He might marry you, if he was a decent, trustworthy sort of bloke, and take you away from it all. You'd be safe enough once you were married.'

My heart lifted slightly. 'But I can hardly ask this man to marry me, can I?'

'Do you *really* love him? Do you want to marry him?'

'I hadn't thought about it till you mentioned it just now,' I said truthfully.

'Who is he? If you've met him since you were here I probably know him.'

'You do,' I said. I stood up and brushed down my dress. 'I've got to go,' I said, but my heart was so full of dread that I didn't think I could move. How was I going to sit and talk to them all as though it was all unchanged? How could I bear to see their faces and keep my thoughts from bursting out of my mouth? 'Well, thanks for the timely warning,' I said drearily.

His hand closed round my ankle. He looked up at me eagerly, 'Judy, who is the man? Tell me.'

But my voice had vanished.

And then he was standing very close to

120

me. 'Darling, I'm almost old enough to be your father.'

'I like mature men,' I said. 'Boys are so silly.'

'That is the only compensation I have ever found for growing old; there's a remote chance that a heavenly princess will fall in love with you for five minutes, and prefer you to a lot of 'silly boys.' Do you mean it, Judy? Will you *promise* to love me till this time tomorrow?'

'I've promised to love you forever, and now you want me to promise for tomorrow too. And you haven't said you love me yet.'

'Love you, you minx? You knew the very first day that I was lost, doomed to walk around for the rest of my life without a heart. I adore you, you're the most ravishing creature that ever was — '

'As beautiful as Olivia Fane?'

'That hag!' he said scornfully.

Then he suddenly became serious again and insisted that he was too old and altogether impossible, unsuitable in every way. He said that he had to take into consideration the fact that if my father were still alive he would definitely disapprove of such a marriage. It was not fair to ignore that, when I was still so very young and inexperienced and had no one I could really trust in to guide me. He had to be both parent and suitor, and it wasn't easy. I said, if he really loved me he jolly well wouldn't stop to put a whole lot of ridiculous obstacles in my way. He felt it was his duty, he said firmly and began quoting that maddening bit, that must have enraged every woman since it was written, about not loving me, dear, so much, loved he not honour more. So I said, Tcha, he wasn't going to marry Father but me, and anyway, I thought the big idea was that I was in mortal danger and that once I was married I would be safe.

Well, he argued a bit more, but that had rather shaken him I could see. He kept asking me if I was absolutely sure I loved him. He seemed to think that the only way to tell if you really loved a person was to have been in love with a whole lot of people before. He had the idea that I was too young to know my own mind. I should think he must have used every argument ever invented.

Then at last he gave in. He just sighed and said, 'Oh, well, that is off my chest, thank goodness! Now I can go ahead and love you all I want.'

And so he did. He kissed me so that I felt I had never been kissed before, even by him . . .

'You'll marry me soon,' he whispered, 'won't you? Not only for that, my precious one, but because I want you so badly that I simply shall not be able to live without you for very long.'

'As soon as possible,' I murmured.

The shadows had crept back to their homes again and the sun was right overhead. I was going to miss luncheon I could see, and I wondered what my family would think; and whether they would worry.

Rex said, 'Don't tell your family, darling. Not yet, anyway. In case they want to make trouble, and they may. It'll be our secret for a bit, eh?'

I agreed of course. Then we went home. I could hardly bear to say good-bye to him. When I went in I thought everyone would be able to read my shining eyes and my mouth that wouldn't stop smiling. I went over it all in my mind, again and again, re-living every little detail, every word and gesture. But it was quite a long time after that I began to wonder how it was Rex knew so much about my family and the terms of my inheritance.

7

The Hut in the Wood

I lived in an incredulous whirl for the next few days. That Rex loved me, actually loved me enough to want to marry me! I simply could not believe it. I kept wondering what on earth he saw in me, and thanking heaven that love is blind. Of course I was crazy to tell someone — I wanted to tell the whole world, and even one person would have been better than nothing, to while away the dreary hours when Rex and I had to be apart. However, I held my peace.

I didn't spend much of the time with my family, anyway. I couldn't feel really at ease with them after what Rex had told me — and who can wonder? Most of the time I spent roaming round the country-side or talking to the village children or the old men, sitting in the sun, fishing. Once or twice I rather shyly called on

Olivia, who seemed always quietly glad to see me, without being in the least gushing about it, and was probably just as quietly glad to see me go. One time I asked her if she thought it was a bad thing to marry a man a lot older than yourself.

'I don't think that sort of thing matters very much if one really and truly loves the man. The main thing is to be very sure that one loves him and will love him forever. Then all the rest is easy.'

'I don't see how one can be *sure* one is going to love someone forever. I mean, that's why there are divorces, aren't there?' I felt rather grown-up and wise when I said that.

'That is because they *weren't* sure, dear. And do *you* feel sure that your love for him is real and lasting?'

'What do you m-mean?' I stammered. 'I never said — '

Her laugh was pretty, like bells. 'Transparent child,' she said. 'You didn't have to say anything when it was written all over your face.'

'Oh!' I blushed. 'And — and do you know who . . . ' I muttered.

'I dare say I could make a guess, but I'd much rather you told me — if you want to; and if you want to keep it a secret I won't try to guess.'

'I'd be glad for you to know. You see, I can't tell my family . . . at — at present, anyway. I think they'd disapprove. And I'm longing to tell about it, it's burning me up,' I said. 'It's Rex — Rex Brady.'

'So you're in love with Rex Brady.' Her smile was slow in coming and even when it did come her eyes remained thoughtful. 'Yes, he is a very attractive man, and he has genuine charm too. I can easily understand his fascination. But you haven't known him very long, dear, and you don't know much about him, do you?'

'I know all the things that count. I may not know the silly things like what he does for a living or how much money he has or who his family were; but I do know that he is kind and brave and thoughtful and amusing.'

'I know he is, my dear. I dare say you think me hard and worldly. And you don't know what I mean when I say you are so young. Be careful, Judith — '

'Oh, *careful!*' I cried scornfully. 'Everybody tells me to be careful. What good does that do? I can't go through life being afraid of the bogey under the bed. Rex loves me and wants to marry me, and why should I always be afraid? Being grown-up isn't much fun if you've always got to be afraid.'

'Being grown-up can be pretty dangerous sometimes,' said Olivia gently. 'But I didn't know he had already proposed to you. That makes a difference, your love being reciprocated. I take back all I said. I wish you every happiness, Judith dear, and I hope soon to congratulate the lucky man. The engagement is to remain a secret, I gather.'

'Oh yes, please, Olivia, promise you won't tell. It would spoil everything if it leaked out, and Rex would be furious with me. He made me promise to keep it a secret. Only I knew I could trust you, and I did so badly want to tell *someone*, and I thought you would be the very person to advise me what to wear.'

'To wear! For the wedding? Oh, there's

plenty of time to discuss that. When have you planned for it to be?'

'It's to be next week. Just as soon as he can get the licence.'

'What!'

'It's to be an elopement, by special licence,' I said proudly. 'We're to meet up in London and be married at St. Mark's. Isn't it fun?'

'Oh, Judith,' she said, reproachfully, 'that isn't the way to get married, in that sneaking, hole-and-corner fashion. Why the hurry?'

'There honestly is a reason for it, though I can't tell you what it is. It is important that we get married right away,' I protested.

She said tenderly, 'You think I'm too old to understand, but I know what it is like to be in love. I know how urgently exciting it all is. But think of other people, think of your mother, my dear, you do owe her something, even if it is only common courtesy. You can't get married without letting her know. It isn't fair, it isn't giving her a chance to put forward her point of view. If she is unreasonable, and you are still of the same mind, then is time enough to think of an elopement. And if you think there is some reason, right or wrong, why she would not accept him, then you know very well that you ought to give her the opportunity to say what she thinks. No, Judith, you can't go through with it. I don't believe in your heart of hearts you even want to.'

'But I do. I thought you'd understand and help. If you knew the facts you would. As it is, we'll just have to leave it at that.'

'Oh no, we can't. I must insist on your telling your mother.'

I shook my head.

'Don't go by me. Ask your sister or your brother if I'm not right.'

'I can't,' I said helplessly, wishing I had never told her.

'I loathe interfering, but I'm afraid that if you don't tell your mother that you want to marry Rex Brady, then I will.'

'Olivia, you wouldn't — you can't,' I said. 'You *promised* me.'

I begged and wheedled in vain. She was adamant.

The end of it was that I told Millicent, of course. I couldn't let her hear it behind my back, even though I didn't think I owed her anything. That was no reason for hurting her. I kept it from Rex for the time being, till I had Mother's reactions. I didn't want two angry people to cope with. However, Mother took it very quietly. She made no fuss at all. She was glad I had told her, she said, but if I really wanted to marry this man she knew that nothing she could say would prevent me. She wasn't going to pretend that she was pleased or that she approved, all the same. She did not consider Rex was a suitable man for me; he was too old and too blasé; and she wanted very much to persuade me to wait till I attained my majority, and knew a bit more about life in general. Marriage lasts a long time, she said.

'So I hope,' I said cheerfully. But this overt disapproval jarred. If they had anything against Rex why didn't they say so, instead, of toadying around with a lot of rot about my being too young to know my own mind. I knew Rex was all right of course, but it made me feel uneasy all the same.

Millicent persuaded me not to elope but to get married here, a proper wedding with white satin and a veil. I thought it was a little soon after Father's death. But she said, nonsense, and the villagers would never forgive me if I didn't do it in style. She said she would arrange it all and that would be fun in compensation for losing me. And then she said, 'Baby!' in that heart breaking voice of hers, and kissed me and said, 'There, run along now.'

On the Sunday she appeared at breakfast most beautifully dressed.

'Who's coming to church with me this morning?' she said gaily.

And we said, 'Church!' in that horrified sort of voice, you know, and flopped back in our chairs with looks of anguish.

'How badly you children have been brought up!' she complained. 'But really, you must come. It's something special, I promise you.'

In the end we all went, and sat fidgeting on the hard wooden pews in the little old church with its cold, dark, vaultings of stone, and listened to the vicar droning as sweetly and unintelligibly as a hiveful of bees. I was almost nodding off to sleep when my name sprang out of the mumble,

' . . . Judith Allen, spinster of this parish . . . why these two should not be joined together . . . This is the first time of asking . . . '

I looked at Millicent and she was laughing silently. The other two looked daft with astonishment. It almost made me laugh too, to see them, but I was angry with Millicent for tricking me so. Rex would not be best pleased, and I was in danger again, which wasn't so jolly. Once the service was over and we were outside again, I had as much envy and congratulation handed to me as I could stomach.

Someone burbled, 'Ah, Mrs. Allen, you've no sooner got your little girlie back than you're to lose her again.' And Mother caught my eye and winked.

When we got back Terry had a 'phone call calling him back to town urgently on some business or another. He shouted at me to come up and talk to him while he threw a few rags into a bag.

I sat on the edge of his bed and listened to him chattering. He was talking to me about my forthcoming marriage, of course, and pretending to be hurt because I hadn't confided in him.

'After all,' he said, 'I practically brought you together when you come to think of it.'

'No, Elsie Thompson did that.'

'That's a sordid way of looking at it. I brought Rex here in the first instance, not Elsie Thompson, poor lass . . . Hullo! And while we're on the subject of death, do I take this with me or not?' He balanced a heavy revolver on his hand thoughtfully.

'Whatever do you want that for, my good boy? You're not a burg-u-lar, are you, or are you?'

'Of course. I'm the Silver Spider, the head of London's most formidable gang, the king of the underworld! That's why I got holes in me socks, I can't get me moll to mend 'em. If you were a sister worth mentioning you'd darn them for me.'

'Oh, fudge!' I said lazily. 'Put ink on your skin and no one'll know.'

'You take it for granted that I have no love-life at all. How am I going to look with nasty blue patches all over my pretty pink skin? She'll think I've got the plague.'

I giggled. 'She will anyway if you go round the place with a damn great pistol.'

'She won't look at me otherwise,' he said sorrowfully. 'But you think I should not take it? Perhaps you're right.' He put it down and went on with his packing. I picked it up and played about with it idly. I squinted down the barrel at Terry. 'Hands up,' I squawked sepulchrally.

'Holy Moses!' he yelled, and jumped to one side. 'It's loaded, you young idiot. You might have killed me.'

'Nonsense. No lady can shoot straight. Everyone knows that.'

I put the gun down and rolled off the bed.

After kissing Terry goodbye, I went off to meet Rex. Rex had not been in church, and I wondered how I was going to tell him that the gaff had been blown. At any moment someone might come along and offer congratulations, and it would be too bad if he was taken unawares.

I was the least little bit afraid of telling him. I picked at his lapel shyly, and looked up at him from under my lashes, the way they do on the screen. 'Promise you won't get mad,' I said.

'My God,' he said, when I had broken it to him. 'That's torn it! Whatever induced you to do a damnfool thing like that?'

'It really did seem rather shabby not to tell anyone.'

'You'll feel shabby, you muggins, if you have to be buried in your wedding-gown.' He put his hand over his eyes. 'We've got to think out some way of circumventing this,' he muttered.

'Circumventing what?'

'I don't know, I don't know. Because my precious girl has gone and chucked a spanner in the works. We'll just have to look lively and think fast . . . oh, I do *wish* you hadn't done it!'

Rex was drumming on the window-pane, with a set and dreary face. I didn't seem to be of any use, so I crept away. My 'so long' was very husky. He didn't turn his head or answer. I don't think he noticed that I wasn't there anymore.

I still felt rather sorry for myself the next day, and I sat moodily chasing an overcooked sausage round my plate. Millicent ripped open a letter and said: 'Oh, lord, if it isn't one damn thing after another,' and tossed it across to me.

It was a typewritten letter from Terry, entirely in lower case giving the news that he had broken his wrist in his right hand. He had slipped and fallen whilst running for a bus. The letter ended:

it is maddeningly incapacitating, if this was written with proper capitals and stops it would not look nearly so silly i assure you. i have no pain dear mother now so there is no need to worry on that score, and apart from a few bruises i am as good as ever i was. enough of this foolishness as nannie used to say when i became restive around six p.m.
your devoted son
X my mark.

I agreed that it really did seem as though fate was goading us with malice, but was glad that Terry was so cheerful. I thought it might be rather fun to go up to town and look him up, and at the same time do a little trousseau shopping. I was going to ask Olivia the best places to go, and perhaps she would give me an introduction to whichever was *the* place for wedding-dresses. Maybe she'd even come with me and help choose, and afterwards we could look up Terry and see if he was quite comfortable. But things arranged themselves differently.

I didn't see Rex the next day, and I thought I would leave it to him to make the first move. He rang me up in the evening and said he had been very busy and he was sorry not to have seen me, and so on.

'Been enjoying yourself, my love?' I said.

'Not pleasure; business — you know. It's boiling up beautifully — just wait till you hear. Can't tell you now naturally. But be ready. And *be* careful — '

'You sound like the Thirty-nine Steps,' I laughed.

'Maybe. But you be ready, won't you, if I need you, sweet? We may fool 'em yet and marry before they're ready for us . . . No, darling, I can't argue about it here and now. You haven't changed your mind, have you? You *do* still love me? Good. Well, you run off to bed now and dream about where you would like to spend your honeymoon . . . Nightie-night, sweet.'

I reminded myself that he had plenty on his mind. We were both feeling the strain of it. If I couldn't *trust* him over a simple thing like this I was going to make a pretty poor sort of wife. I wondered just what he had been doing, and whether we would elope after all?

One funny thing had happened though, that hadn't seemed important enough to tell Rex. My diary was missing. I always kept it in the same place, right by my bed, so that I could write in it last thing at night. But I couldn't find it anywhere. It was a nuisance, because I have kept a diary ever since I was a kid, and just jotted down reminders of what has happened during the day. There was nothing startling or even interesting in it for anyone else. That's why I didn't worry about it disappearing, because it couldn't have any importance for anyone else, and it was merely a nuisance for me personally to be without it. But it was a mystery nevertheless.

The maids, of course, knew nothing about it when I asked them. And when I tackled Millicent, she stared at me mistily for a long while and finally went off on a ramble about casting horoscopes for racehorses. 'I see the *whole* thing now. I've been an absolute fool! It's not a bit of use casting horoscopes of the jockeys alone; I must do the horses too. Obviously!'

So it wasn't much use talking to her. I said, 'What about the owners and the trainers and all the whole boiling of them?' feeling spiteful.

The next day brought a note from Rex, asking me to meet him that afternoon in the hut in the wood. I knew where he meant. The woods were on the side of

Breem Hill, where we had been the day he proposed to me, and on the edge of them was a small, disused, forester's cabin. We had made up foolish fairy tales about it, the way one does.

It was all very secretive and mysterious, but I didn't suppose he would be so roundabout without some good reason, and so it wasn't hard to guess that he was on the track of something or other. I decided that if he really had been doing good work I would forgive him his coolness towards me.

In the middle of luncheon I was suddenly pierced by a knife-like intuition. The whole note was a fake! I could hardly prevent myself from leaving the table there and then and taking another peek at it. What had it said?

'Come to the little hut this afternoon at three. This is very important, darling. I have found out you know what, but do not want to put it down on paper. For goodness' sake, do not tell anyone where you are going or that you are meeting me. — REX.'

That was more or less how it ran, if not

word for word. And if that didn't smell fishy I'm a vegetarian. That, 'Don't tell anyone' touch! Why, it was exactly the kind of thing one has read a hundred times, where the innocent heroine goes bouncing off full of girlish laughter and walks smack into the trap that was plainer than a pikestaff to everyone else — and serve her right.

Luncheon over, I went to find that note, and believe it or not, the damned thing had vanished. Well, that, thought I, was very *odd*, but perhaps only to be expected. And where does one go from here? I asked myself. Of course! Ring Rex and find out what he thought on the matter. So I did. I listened to the bell pealing its double ring in the distance for a long while, and then I put down the receiver. I looked at my watch: it was 2 p.m. He might have left for the wood already. I might be mistaken, and the note had come from him after all. Perhaps I was being melodramatic, thinking in terms of villains, spies, and traps. And yet, the more commonsense argued with me the more intuition insisted that I was right. Well, either way, I was going to find out. I climbed upstairs slowly, thinking.

I couldn't imagine what sort of trap would be awaiting me at the top of the hill, or who would be there to receive me, but I didn't intend to be taken by surprise. I made my plans — such as they were — while I dressed. It puzzled me where the note could have got to, and I wished I had it. When I was ready I went into Terry's room to look for the revolver. There it was waiting for me, on the top of his chest of drawers where he had left it. I didn't know how you opened the thing to see if it was loaded, but it felt as heavy as before, so I concluded it was. It was a comforting kind of companion, anyway, I thought, as I slipped it into my big leather bag.

For once I did feel like someone on the films, very grim and self-reliant. I pulled my hat down and strode from the house without anyone seeing me. I went as fast as I could; it would take me all of half an hour, to get there, and it looked as though it might rain.

When I drew near, I paused to get my

breath and lessen the excited beating of my heart. Now that I was actually there, for two pins I would have turned round and gone home — and didn't I just wish I had afterwards! I took the revolver out of my bag. I held it so that it felt snug and homely in my hand, with my forefinger stroking the trigger very lightly. I walked quietly forward.

The door of the hut was ajar. I waited, but no sound came from inside. I kicked the door wide with my foot, keeping the gun as steady as I could, breast-high. Nothing. It was dark in the hut and from the threshold I couldn't make out anything inside. Then I saw Rex's panama hat, a familiar white blur on the floor. I stooped and picked it up wonderingly. There was a dark stain on the side of it — which should have warned me.

At the back of the hut, against the wall, was a bench. I could see a dark sort of blodge on it now, and I went over to it. Someone was piled tidily along it. I didn't need to look twice even in that dim light to see who it was. I put the revolver back in my bag because I wasn't going to need it now.

I touched Rex gently, but I knew he was quite dead, before I did so, by the great stain clotting his shirt front and spattering down his trousers on to the floor. His white teeth grinned at me from his upturned face.

'Oh, Rex,' I moaned, remembering his kisses, remembering his kindness and courage and how he had saved me from drowning, remembering all his warning remarks, and how in spite of that I had given the game away, and he had paid the penalty by walking into the trap laid for me — so for the last time he had saved my life and this time at the expense of his own. I didn't know how I was going to be able to bear that knowledge for the rest of my life.

Virtually, I had killed him, I kept repeating to myself dully. Yes, but not actually, came the realisation. Somebody else had pulled the trigger or plunged the knife, or whatever it was that killed him. The thought was like a stab of lightning, jerking me awake. Rex had been *murdered!* And I was standing there like a dummy! Supposing someone were to walk in quite casually and find me there?

I was out of there as fast as Lucifer falling from heaven, shaking all over. There was the beastly feeling that the murderer might be hanging around somewhere in the vicinity. My one desire was to get away from there as fast as possible, but I was almost half-way down the hill when I discovered that I was still stupidly clutching Rex's bloodstained Panama hat in my hand.

I stood there on the narrow track between the trees and thought out what I should do. To take the hat home with me and to try and dispose of it there by burning it up, for instance, might involve me in all manner of complications. The point that I had realized with bitterness and shame was that I could not afford to have my name brought into this. I had to do a very blackguardly thing if I wished Rex's murderer to be caught, and that was to feign entire ignorance of the occurrence. I had to leave my poor dead lover alone up there until he was discovered in the course of time by someone else. If it seemed like a betrayal, I hoped Rex would understand. Not for me the relief of informing the police and having the onus taken from me. Nor for me the satisfaction of acceptable grief, open and unashamed. I realized that now Rex had gone I really was alone in my battle of wits and guile and strength. What *could* I do with this hat? If I flung it away somewhere beneath a clump of bushes it might not be found, and who knows what incriminating evidence lay in it to the discerning eye. That decided me. I went back, up the steep path to the hut, and in, with clenched jaw, to deposit the hat on the floor where I had found it. Then I was free again and running down the slope . . .

But I had lost valuable time. I tried, as I ran, to control my tumultuous thoughts and figure out some kind of an alibi for myself. And all the while I saw Rex's dead and livid face before me.

The rain I had been expecting came down as if someone had pulled the plug out of the bottom of the bathtub up there. I was sopping wet in a few minutes.

I climbed over the wall and came round to the side of the house. The drawing-room was empty, and I took off my dirty shoes and crept through up to my room. Then I quickly stripped off my wet clothes and stepped into a hot bath. I lay there, shuddering with reaction, till the hot water relaxed my limbs and soothed my nerves into drowsy warmth . . .

An incessant rhythm in my brain demanded, 'When will Rex be found . . . ? Who will find him . . . ? When will Rex be found . . . ?'

8

Enter Amy Garnet

It was curious to consider that everything went on just the same, and Rex being dead didn't make a particle of difference. Even while he was actually being killed other people had been living their normal life quite close at hand. Millicent had spent the afternoon happily poring over her horoscopes, and Toni had gone to Garthurst in the car to see a flick. All just as though murder was not stalking abroad almost beneath their eyes.

I rang Olivia, but she was still out.

The sun was hanging just above the clump of elms that fixed the western boundary of our estate, when there was a squeal of brakes and the whine of tyres brought to a stand still too suddenly on the gravel drive. I watched Olivia swing out of her car with a lithe movement and race up the steps like a girl. I realized that imagining I could confide in her was wishful thinking. Mine was a secret that had to be kept.

She said, 'Sweet, I've only popped in for a minute on my way home, because I'm absolutely *dropping*, and if you offered me a drink it would be a charity.'

'You look anything but dropping,' I remarked, as I mixed her a drink.

'I feel like a dead rat, I assure you. In town all day. Working like a lunatic this morning and rushed all the work through so that I could lunch with your brother and be with him this afternoon. Which is why I'm here now, if you get me; to give you his love and to tell you that he is going along nicely and the doctor says he is a good boy, and he hopes to come down in a few days — Terry, not the doctor. Here's how!' She raised her glass. 'My own wrist feels almost broken from all the stenographing I've done on his behalf. You're looking rather peaky, child,' she remarked presently, when she had reported a lot of nonsense from Terry. 'What's the matter?'

'Nothing,' I said. 'Do I? I haven't been

out today, I expect I need some air.'

She looked at me sharply. 'Not had a lover's quarrel or anything like that?'

I said gaily, 'Wishful thinking, you nasty girl?' And thought what a good actress I was. 'As a matter of fact, I haven't seen anything of Rex for a couple of days. He's been busy . . . such a lot to do . . . we're going to be married quite soon, you know.' And then in a rush, 'Oh, Olivia, I thought maybe you'd help me get my trousseau — oh, I don't mean all the palaver, but come with me to choose the dress and that. I don't know whether Millicent would be offended, but she hasn't got your taste.' I heard myself quacking feebly on and on. But Olivia did not seem to notice that anything was amiss.

We discussed clothes for a little while longer and then she protested that she really must go before she fell asleep where she was. She kissed me good-bye. 'Take care of yourself, pretty pet, and don't let Rex wear you out.'

I stayed up as late as I could that night, talking, and when the others retired, I went to my room but I didn't undress. I sat on the end of the bed, longing for day. It was a haunted night even with the light on. Rex seemed to be reproaching me, he seemed to think it was my fault that he was lying there cold and dead. I thought that now I was alone I could cry for him, but I couldn't. The source of my tears seemed to have dried up. I felt empty of everything except a kind of dreary, frightened waiting. *Had* I done right not to go to the police?

Then I pulled myself together and tried to put a face on the formless creeping murderer. Who could it have been? Was there anyone who wanted to get rid of me *except* my family? Only those in some intimate connection with my family — as far as I knew. Well, then — no flinching — let us examine their alibis — for what they were worth.

Millicent had been in her boudoir, hadn't she? Or had she? Come to think of it, if I could sneak in and out of the house unseen, presumably another person could. But could she have moved up that hill ahead of me, killed Rex and made her getaway before I appeared on the scene? Or had she remained in hiding up there till I had been and gone? But then why not have disposed of me and made it appear to be a suicide pact, or some such nonsense? I didn't even know if there was a hiding-place up there, or how Rex had been killed. I didn't know anything, and I hadn't had the wit to try and use my eyes when I was up there. I was a lousy detective!

I considered Toni. Now, surely Toni was all right, or was the car-ride to the cinema at Garthurst a blind? Was it a fake alibi too? It ought to be a fairly simple matter to time the drive there and check up with the time on the ticket-stub. If that fitted it surely must be all right, because Toni had left the house after I did. But there was the possibility that she had wangled something with Curdie, though I didn't see how. It meant, though, that I would have to investigate Curdie's alibi. I wished I knew how I was going to do all this. It all sounded very easy when it was the detective who went round — he always knew where to go — and asked the questions —

and he always knew the right questions to ask too. Of course, being a detective probably made it come easier; the official status would give him a certain kudos. On the other hand, I consoled myself, there must be many advantages in playing a lone, hidden hand. Lone-Wolf Allen, the Two-Gun Girl of Bar X, that was me. Well, who else was there to consider?

Terry was pretty well out of the running, being in London and with Olivia most of the time, and anyway, his wrist was broken.

Neville was next on the list then. What had he been doing? Something on or for the estate almost certainly. But strolling from one group of workers to another, or sitting in his office totting up columns of figures, wasn't going to cover him very securely, he would need to find something better than that. There were too many loopholes for him to slip through in that sort of alibi. He was busy overseeing the workers; but who was overseeing him? Who would notice if he slipped way for an hour? I remembered that Latin tag they taught us in school that always made my knees shake with its eeriness: Who watches the custodians? *Quis custodiet ipsos custodes?* Neville Thompson's activities that day would need carefully looking into.

I switched off the light. The first cold light of morning shuddered greyly across the sky. I was thoroughly tired. I yawned and shivered. Then I stripped off my clothes and left them lying on the floor guiltily, and tumbled into bed. I fell dreamlessly asleep at once.

I was awakened by the little housemaid shaking me timidly and repeating loudly, 'There's a lady to see you, Miss . . . '

The sun flooded across my bed. I said sleepily, 'What's the time?'

'Gone ten, Miss . . . I told the lady you was sleeping, but she says it was important and she'd wait . . . She's been waiting a bit already . . . so I thought I'd better see if you was awake yet.' She stood there anxiously, her hands at her side as she had been taught.

'That's all right, Lucy.' I threw back the clothes and swung out of bed. 'Who is the lady?'

'I don't know her by sight, Miss, not

from these parts. She told me her name — Mrs. Gurney, or some such. I forget.'

'Oh, hell! Didn't you ask her what she wanted?' I buckled on a pair of striped sandals.

'She wouldn't say, Miss — only that it was important. Shall I tell cook to get your breakfast ready, Miss?'

'No, never mind it. You must *always* find out what people want, Lucy. Did she ask for me specially, or the lady of the house?'

'She says, I want to see Miss Judith Allen. Just like that, Miss . . . '

I couldn't place anyone called Gurney, or anything like it. I combed my hair into place and made up my face automatically. I hurried downstairs.

A short woman was standing at the library window when I came in. She turned and watched me walking towards her with outstretched hand. She was not young, nor pretty, but dark and dowdily dressed. I thought perhaps she had come to sell something. There was a little suitcase by her side.

I said, 'Good morning. I must apologise for keeping you waiting, Mrs. — er — '

'Mrs. Garnet,' she said. Her voice was low and lady-like. 'Are you Miss Judith Allen?'

'Yes. Won't you sit down?' I perched on the arm of a chair. But she remained standing stiffly. 'What can I do for you?'

'Miss Allen, where is my husband?'

She kind of spat the words out of her mouth in her hurry to get rid of them. I wanted to laugh, it sounded so absurd.

'I'm afraid I can't tell you. I haven't the pleasure of Mr. Garnet's acquaintance.'

'Oh, but you have' — I wondered whether she was mildly insane — 'only, you don't know him as Mr. Garnet. You think he's called Rex Brady . . . '

'But Rex can't be your husband, he's going to marry me. There must be some mistake,' I said stupidly.

'There is no mistake, Miss Allen. Look!' She fumbled in her bag and brought out a piece of paper which she handed to me. I noticed that her gloved hands were shaking. The paper had cut out letters of unequal sizes pasted on to form a message. I stared at it, but my eyes made no attempt to read the words. My thoughts were spinning crazily, and I was trying desperately to make them function again quickly and smoothly as usual: I knew I had to think fast; but I couldn't think at all, my mind was a blank. The blood in my ears kept throbbing: '*Danger . . . danger . . . danger . . .* ' I stood up and walked over to the window with the piece of paper. It read:

WHAT IS HUBBY UP TO? THE VICAR OF OLD LANGTON WILL TELL YOU. ASK ABOUT MR. BRADY. — A PAL.

She came and stood beside me, her face expressionless.

'That's what I got,' she said dully. 'I had my own reasons for not ignoring, it. Things hadn't been right at home for quite a while; but I don't want to go into all that now. So I came down this morning by the first train, and I went to see the vicar, and he told me about this

Mr. Brady, as he calls himself, and you, Miss Allen, and how the banns had been put up for the first time last week. Then, I knew I had to stop it. I couldn't have him doing it again. It's not right. The vicar gave me his address, and I came down to see him straight away. But he wasn't there. I saw the woman who does for him. She said he hadn't been in all night, his bed hadn't been slept in, and the supper she had prepared the day before had not been touched. He hadn't told her he was going away or anything, nor had he taken a suitcase with him. Well, all that means nothing to me, I don't know what his habits are,' she said with a trace of bitterness. 'But the woman told me that he had a note yesterday morning, and he had gone straight out after receiving it. And presumably never returned . . . I thought *you* might know something . . . ' Her monotonous voice trailed into silence expectantly.

'What should I know?' I heard myself say remotely.

'You were to be his future wife. You would have been if — '

'*Would* have been?' I stammered. 'If, what? What do you mean?'

'If I hadn't been warned, of course.'

'But it's all too utterly fantastic,' I cried suddenly. 'Who *are* you? I've never seen you before, and you come down here with this incredible rigmarole to me — to me. What proof have you of — ?'

'Oh, if it's proof you want,' she said, with a tight little smile. She opened her bag again. 'Perhaps you'd care to see my marriage lines,' she said, handing me a paper, soiled at the folds and worn.

The Marylebone Town Hall . . . It was dated November 1935 . . . the registrar . . . the clerk . . . witnesses . . . Then the signatures, Amy Irene Frost and Graham Garnet . . .

I said, 'But my good woman, this only proves you are married to someone called Graham Garnet; but it's nothing to do with Rex Brady. I think you must be mad. You're acting on an anonymous letter. And even that doesn't say that Brady is your husband: it tells you to ask about Mr. Brady. Well, you have. But it hasn't proved anything. You must see that . . .

Anyway, I fail to see that it is anything to do with me.' I walked to the door firmly and opened it. 'If you have lost your husband why don't you go to the police, Mrs. Garnet, they are the proper people to give you the information you need, and they will help you find him. Good-bye, Mrs. Garnet.'

'You may not care to admit it yet, Miss Allen, but it is the truth. I would never have come all this way unless I had been sure. Didn't that anonymous warning have the ring of truth in it?'

'I wouldn't know,' I said coldly. 'I am not in the habit of receiving anonymous letters.'

'You would be if you had married Rex Brady,' she said again in that bitter little voice. 'You see, I've been through this before, Miss Allen. Never mind. Will you tell me when you last saw Mr. Brady?'

'I don't see that it is any of your business. But I'll tell you. I haven't seen him for three days, as it happens.'

'Then you never saw him yesterday after all. What prevented you?' There was a veiled sneer in her tone that I found hard to understand.

'What — what do you mean,' I stammered, 'prevented me?'

'Prevented you from meeting him at the hut as you had arranged,' she explained patiently.

I was dull with sudden fear. Who was this woman? How much did she know? 'The hut?' I repeated inanely.

'The hut, yes, the hut,' she mimicked, like an irritated schoolmistress.

'I don't know what you're talking about.'

'It's very simple, Miss Allen. Graham left your loving little letter behind him and the char showed it to me.' She laughed shortly and unemotionally. 'However, you evidently have your own reasons for not being frank with me. That's your business. But I really do want to see Graham rather badly, so I think I will take your advice and go to the police. I am sure they will be interested in your letter too. You must forgive me for taking up so much of your time. Good-bye, Miss Allen.'

'Wait a moment,' I said. 'I never wrote

to him yesterday. What letter are you talking about? Please let me see it.'

She put her head on one side and looked at me. 'I'll be delighted to show it to you — at the police station.' She raised her eyebrows. 'No? You don't care to accompany me? I thought not, somehow.' She inclined her head at me again, and was gone.

I told myself that it was a gigantic bluff. Some curious kind of blackmail, whose gist I had not yet fully understood. Whoever she was really, she must somehow be aware that Rex was dead and was trying to blackmail me about it because I had not informed the police. That bit about the letter was obviously a shot in the dark because *I had not* written one . . . But there must be more to it than that, I realized, with a shiver. Why all the elaborate story about Rex being her husband? Rex a bigamist! But the idea of him marrying that uninteresting little dowd was even more ridiculous . . . She hadn't identified Rex yet. And Rex was dead. What did that add up to? I wondered. But I couldn't concentrate on it, I was feeling horribly empty inside, and I remembered that I had had no breakfast. I found myself a glass of milk and gulped it down.

Then I went down to Rex's bungalow. The 'daily' was still there, though taking off her apron as I came in.

'Oh, Mrs. Naldicott,' I said. 'Who was that lady who came here this morning? What did she want?'

'Search me,' said Mrs. Naldicott obligingly. 'Nosy old devil, weren't she? Made out she was a relation of the boss's, and the questions she arst, you'd never believe.'

'Did you tell her anything about me? I ask, because she came up to see me afterwards, and I had quite a job to get rid of her.'

'Ar, she said she was going up to you. Well, I didn't really tell her nothing about you, Miss. She seemed like to know already, only she arst what you looked like and all that. I told her you was like one of these young madams on the films that lark about with nothing on. Cor, you should have seen her face, proper study it was, Miss, she weren't arf wild.'

Mrs. Naldicott chuckled at the memory.

'Very naughty, Mrs. Naldicott! And what did you tell her about Mr. Rex not being here? Something about a letter?'

Mrs. Naldicott looked blank.

I felt more hopeful. 'She said you had given her a letter written by me to Mr. Rex,' I elaborated. Maybe the woman *had* invented the letter.

'Oh yes, Miss. We was talking about him not having come in all night and how it wasn't usual, not without letting me know. And I told her how a letter had come for him just as I was preparing a bit of lunch for him. And he says to me not to bother as he's going out. And out he goes. See? So she says, quick as you like, what about that letter? And I let slip, careless-like, that I had seen him leave it behind him. She was on to that like Jack Robinson and had whisked it out of his desk before I could turn round . . . Well, what could I do, Miss? Weren't my place to say nothing, not if she was a relation and all.'

'What made you think the letter came

from me, Mrs. Naldicott?'

'Oh, that! Mr. Rex had left it lying on the desk and I went to tidy it safely away for him and I couldn't help seeing who it was from accidentally. I wouldn't never have thought no more of it, not being one to pry, but she — '

'I'm sure she made it worth your while, Mrs. Naldicott,' I said wearily, and walked away. There was nothing further I could say or do.

If Mrs. Garnet had gone to the police station as she had threatened, she would have told her story by now, and soon — soon they would be investigating the hut ... And what then? I wondered faintly.

I sat down to luncheon and listened to Toni and Millicent bickering about something or another.

Millicent said, 'You're looking ghastly, child.'

'Ructions with Rex,' Toni mouthed knowingly to mother.

'No,' I said, dragging my mouth into a smile. 'I haven't seen him.'

'Well, don't look so miserable, my pet,

you're not going to be hanged. If you've changed your mind and you don't want to marry him, you needn't,' said Millicent soothingly. 'Yes, what is it?' she asked the maid beside her.

'If you please, M'm, there's a policeman . . . He wants to see Miss Judith — '

I scraped my chair back noisily from the table and stood up.

'Guess I must have been driving on the wrong side of the road or something. Well, here goes . . . Excuse me, Mother.'

The policeman was standing in the hall, waiting. It was Babyface, looking very massive. I took him into the library where we could be alone and not overheard.

'Very sorry to disturb you during your meal, Miss,' he began.

'It doesn't matter in the least,' I assured him. 'How can I help you?'

'Well, it's rather awkward, Miss . . . A lady came down to the station this morning and said her husband was missing, and would we please find him for her. Well, of course, the gentleman may have wanted a quiet little trip on his own, but that's none of our business; we have to follow up these suggestions, if they seem reasonable. He's only been missing twenty-four hours, so I dare say he'll stroll in and surprise his good lady any time now. But she was proper worried about him, walking out of the house in the clothes he stood up in, just before his dinner, and never coming back. That was the last that's been seen of him . . . It seems it was a letter he received that made him walk out like that.' He blinked. 'A letter from you, Miss. So I thought I'd just trot up and see if you could tell us anything that might be helpful about it.'

'I never wrote to him,' I said. 'There's some mistake.'

'You know what gentleman I'm talking about, Miss?'

'Oh yes. You mean Mr. Brady, don't you? That woman called on me first of all. I couldn't tell her anything, and it was I who advised her to try the police.'

'Ah,' he said, and took out his notebook and pencil, 'thank you, Miss. Glad to have that corroborative evidence. She said she'd been here. But it's funny about that letter, isn't it, signed Judy and all?'

'She showed it to you?'

'Oh yes. I have it here. Would you care to see it?'

He unbuttoned the breast-pocket of his tunic and selected a sheet of paper. He held it out to me. It danced up and down before my startled eyes, a brief scrawl of words in my own, thin, bright blue handwriting, signed with my own signature . . .

'But it's my writing,' I gasped. 'But I swear I never wrote it. It's a hoax.'

He tucked it away, without speaking. He sighed.

'It's a funny business, Miss.'

'It's utterly fantastic, Constable . . . You know this woman had some story — quite incredible — that Mr. Brady was her husband under another name, Garnet or something . . . Perhaps she's a little crazy, do you think?'

'No, Miss,' said Babyface sadly. 'We turned up the records. Graham Garnet was quite a notorious bigamist . . . served a term in '37. This one is his real wife, his first one, that is. Love is a funny thing, Miss; there's this woman of his following him about everywhere, crazy about him, though she knows he only married her for her savings and he's never been what you'd call faithful to her. You'd think she'd turn nasty, wouldn't you? I'm sorry, Miss, this is painful to you, perhaps?'

'It's all right, Constable. Are you certain that my fiancé is Graham Garnet?'

'We've checked up on that already, Miss.' He looked at me sympathetically. 'Well, that's that. You haven't seen the gentleman in question, don't know anything about this here note, and can't throw any light on his whereabouts?' He scored a heavy line with his pencil and snapped the notebook shut. 'Then I won't trouble you any longer, Miss. Thanking you . . . ' He stood up.

'What happens next?' I said, as we walked to the front door. 'Have you thought of looking up at this hut place?'

He looked at me. His eyes were blue, guileless, and faintly surprised.

'Oh yes, Miss. That has been done.'

He had gone; and I was alone.

9

Rex Is Found

They had finished eating when I returned to the dining-room.

'We thought you'd been jailed,' Toni greeted me. 'What did they want?'

'It was about Rex. He's turned up missing, and his wife wants to know what he's been up to and seems to think I should know ... No, I won't have any fruit, thank you.'

I thought I had better tell them right away. They both seemed genuinely sorry about it. But I was all on edge, waiting to hear officially about Rex's death and what they thought about it. It was while I was telling the twice-told tale and letting the other part of my mind fret over the more secret side of it, that I suddenly recalled with some horror that Terry's gun was still in my handbag. Supposing the police took it into their heads to pay me another visit right away? I had to get rid of that, fast.

'It's no use talking about it, my dears. I don't know any more than I've told you. We'll have to wait and see what transpires.'

'The swine!' said Millicent fiercely. 'If I ever get my hands on him I'll kill him. Supposing he'd married you? Think of that!' she cried with a shudder.

'Thank goodness you discovered it in time,' said Toni.

As soon as I was alone once more, I bolted upstairs and rummaged for my bag, found the revolver still lying inside it. I decided that I couldn't do better than put it back where I found it. With the bag under my arm, I slipped down the corridor to Terry's room. I took out the revolver and left it on top of the chest of drawers, exactly where I had found it. I snapped the bag shut. I could breathe more freely now. Then I went back to my room, wondering what one did on hearing of the sudden death of one's fiancé. Soon now someone was going to break the news to me, and I had to appear as natural as possible..

I stared at myself in the mirror and made a few experimental grimaces at myself in the glass. I flung up my hands in horror. I pressed the back of one hand against my mouth, closed my eyes, and lolled my head backwards, swaying faintly. I tried to cry — but couldn't. Nothing looked right, they looked forced and ridiculous. I hoped that something would help me when the time came, that was all.

I couldn't mourn for Rex. I knew now that he had never really loved me at all. That had just been his line. And no wonder, I thought bitterly, he had been so anxious to save my life and warn me against the other people who were after my money. God forbid anyone else should get their hands on the gold he wanted. Only, his way of getting it was by preserving my life. Perhaps later, though, I would have been induced to make a will in his favour, and then I might have been quietly disposed of. Anyone, it seemed, would murder you for twopence. There was going to be a lot to look forward to in my life, I could see. I wished that Father hadn't cursed me with all that money.

'That copper's back again, Miss.' The little maid startled me out of my reverie.

'The sergeant wondered if you'd mind stepping down to the station for a minute . . . Won't keep you any time . . . Got the car here, Miss . . . '

The sergeant stood up when I came in and offered me a chair deferentially. 'Sorry to bother you, Miss Allen. It's a matter of identification . . . I'm afraid I have to tell you that Mr. Brady has been found, but he had been dead for some hours already . . . Would you like a little water, Miss? This must be a terrible shock for you.'

'I'm all right, thanks.

'I'm afraid we need a formal identification before the post-mortem . . . Take your time, there's no hurry. I only wish I needn't trouble you.'

'I'm ready,' I said.

The sergeant conducted me into the little room with the cold, northern light that I had been in once before. This time, too, a body lay beneath a sheet on the long table by the window. They pulled the sheet away from his face. He looked truly dead now, with his face smoothed into its last mask, from when he had grinned up at me from his huddle on the bench.

I said, 'Yes, that's Rex Brady,' and turned away.

When I was back in the office part of the station, I said, 'What did he die of?'

The sergeant coughed. 'We'll have to wait for the autopsy before we can say exactly. Yes . . . This little puzzle of the note, now . . . curious, that — in your writing but not written by you . . . Mmm, Mmm! And he went up there . . . and died. Yes. But you did not go there . . . Perhaps you were busy,' he suggested.

I shrugged carelessly. 'I don't remember doing anything in particular. I couldn't know that he was going to be killed that day, could I?'

'Killed?' said the sergeant. 'I never said he had been killed.'

'Didn't you?' I said stupidly. 'I suppose I just took it for granted that he was too healthy and normal to die suddenly otherwise.'

'Very,' said the sergeant, staring at me stolidly.

'There's been so much talk of sudden death lately. That actress, Major Thompson's daughter, you know, and all that — ' I ended vaguely.

'Yes,' he agreed. 'You've had quite an eventful time since you've been over here, haven't you? Must make you feel you're back in America with all those gangsters and G-men.'

'I don't ever remember seeing as much blood in America as I've seen here,' I said.

'There was a lot of blood with Mr. Brady, wasn't there?' he acquiesced.

'Blood? Was there? I don't know,' I stuttered. 'I was talking metaphorically of course. Was there a — a lot of blood?'

'Fair amount, considering that death must have been pretty nearly instantaneous. I should think whoever did it must have got their share of it, at that range . . . Well, well, I don't want to bother you with these nasty details, do I? Only so sorry I had to ask you down for the identification.'

I said, 'By the way, does Mrs. — er — Garnet know?'

'Ah, poor lady, she took on terribly. Properly cut up, she was. Must have been very fond of him . . . Oh yes, before I forget . . . what did you say you were doing when he was killed?'

'I don't know when it was,' I reminded him sharply.

'Mmm, nor you do. Suppose you just run through the whole day — if you don't mind, that is. Purely routine, you know.'

I leant back and gave him a résumé that was true in the main, except for the made-up part when I was actually at the hut. I said I'd been writing letters then and afterwards gone to post them and got caught in the rain, come home and had a bath, and so on.

He listened patiently and asked if there was anyone who could corroborate this. I said unfortunately no. What was I wearing? Did I remember? Possibly someone might remember having seen me in the village, posting the letters. I described what I had been wearing, and he wrote it all down. He tossed the list across to Babyface, who promptly vanished with it.

'Well, there you are, Miss. Mmm! Did he seem to be worried about anything recently?'

'Yes.' The sergeant sat up. 'But about me not about himself. He had the idea I was in danger.'

'Were you really in any danger, do you think?'

'I'm not so sure now.' I gnawed at my thumb thoughtfully. 'It sounded very real when he spoke about it, but it occurs to me now that it might be his beastly invention . . . I think — I think he had planned that if I would not marry him for love I would marry him for protection. I know he was very angry with me for telling my family I was going to marry him; he intended to run away with me and marry me quickly and secretly.'

The sergeant shook his head ruefully, 'What a nasty bit of work, he was. But you don't believe this danger you were supposed to be in could have been — well, equally dangerous to him, shall we say?'

'Oh no. It was purely personal danger.'

'Ah, yes, I see,' said the sergeant, in a wise voice. 'And he didn't seem worried apart from that? Had he any enemies that you know of?'

'He *did* seem worried about something — I hardly saw him the last few days, it's true, but it was because he was busy and anxious, I thought — and all the time I thought it was something to do with me; but I see now that it may not have been . . . As for enemies, I should think a man of his habits would have plenty, but you would know more about that than I would. His wife seemed very anxious about him all of a sudden,' I added casually.

'Ah, she knew his little games, Miss. She wanted to prevent him committing bigamy again.'

'That's her story,' I said lightly. 'She needn't have bothered herself though. He was dead already when she came down, wasn't he?'

Babyface came in and passed a slip of paper to his superior officer. The sergeant put on a pair of pince-nez and stared at it.

Then he leant back in his chair, removed his glasses and looked at me mildly with some reproach.

'You never told me you'd been up to the hut, Miss Allen.'

I could feel the colour spreading across my face like a flag.

'What makes you say that?'

The sergeant laughed gently. 'Oh, come! We're not trying to trip you up, you know. We don't go in for Scotland Yard methods here. Why innocent people will try to hide things when they haven't anything to hide, I don't know. They make our work doubly hard. And they often cover up valuable clues until it's too late. Then the police get blamed for not solving the crimes. All this because people are afraid and selfish and don't *think!*' He stared at me accusingly. 'Did you really imagine that we should not find out?'

I said I was sorry. 'But how did you find out, anyway?'

'Footprints, my dear young lady. Footprints that fitted neatly your little tan crepe-soled shoes,' he smirked.

'But it rained, after that,' I said.

180

'Not *inside* the hut — and there was some blood on the crepe . . . Now, suppose you tell me what really happened?'

'I *did* go up there. I had a note, you see, telling me to be there at three o'clock without fail. It was in Rex's handwriting, but it — it didn't ring quite true somehow. I went there, all the same. When I got there he was lying dead inside the hut already. There was no mistake about that. I didn't touch anything, except his hat. I picked that up off the floor as I went in, without thinking, not knowing that I was going to see his dead body in half a minute. I left then, and I was more than half-way home when I realized that I was still clutching that damned hat. I thought it might be a clue or something so I took it back and put it where I had found it. Then I came away.'

'But why on earth did you not notify us at once? Surely you must have known it was your duty to do so?'

'I suppose it was very wrong of me. I — I didn't want to get mixed up in it. I didn't understand. I thought then that it was something to do with me; I even thought that perhaps in some strange way he had been killed in mistake for me; and so I thought it was safer for me to lie low for a while, and that I would have more chance of finding out the real criminal that way. I can see now that I was wrong, and I really am sorry for the inconvenience I have caused,' I said meekly.

He let it go at that. 'Might I see this note that purported to come from him?'

'Willingly, if I had it. The funny thing is, I put it down somewhere for a minute, and when I came to look for it again it had gone. I suppose a maid picked it up off the floor and threw it away as rubbish. Curious, though.'

'Very curious,' he commented seriously. 'Do you recall what it said.'

'I think I can: 'Be at the little hut at three p.m. today. I have found out something very important, darling, but I do not care to write it. Whatever you do, don't tell anyone where you are going to meet me. — REX.' As near as I can remember.'

'I see. And so you went — not expecting to find him dead.'

'Not even expecting to find him at all, to be quite frank. I imagined a trap.'

'It would have been wiser to come to us.'

'Oh yes, you always say that afterwards; never before. If nothing had come of it, you would have been just as peeved.'

'But Garnet might have been alive.'

'Oh, quite. And in jail. Or I might have been married to a bigamist. Anyway, what is the use of brooding about it now?'

'No. What's been done can't be undone, as they say. So we'll let it go at that — for the time being. You won't be leaving the neighbourhood at present, will you?' He stood up.

I rose too. 'Not that I know of.'

'It's a simple matter of official convenience to keep the witnesses together on a case, nothing more,' he said soothingly.

I went straight home. As I came in, Toni came up through a trap-door in the floor like the demon-king in a pantomime.

'Where on earth have you come from?'

'The dark-room.' And at my look of surprise, she said, 'Didn't you know I was interested in photography? Get exhibited at all the posh shows, I do. I've a dark-room in the cellar. I find it pays every time to develop your own stuff; then you get exactly what you want.'

'I'd love to see your stuff, Toni.'

'So you shall, my dear. A lot of it's very modern, you know. That's the part I'm interested in. You can get curious effects with a camera that you can get no other way. I want to try it out on the stage — when Curdie and I have our experimental theatre.' She led me downstairs where, next to the tiny dark-room, part of the cellar had been whitewashed and rigged up with good lighting apparatus. Photographs, mounted and unmounted, were pinned against the wall or lay neatly filed in boxes stacked on the table.

Some of them were a little crazy. Photos of Millicent taken at queer angles and with every strange type of lighting you could imagine. There was a photo of Terry I rather liked, the back of his head and one hand, writing in Greek on the sand with his finger. There were a few exquisite views. A terrifying close-up of an orchid. Some alarming interiors, like something out of the 'Cabinet of Dr. Caligari.' A boxful of stage-sets designed by her, some of them models, some of them taken on an actual stage. Among the photos of people was one that arrested my attention as I flicked through them. It was of a girl, and there was something vaguely familiar about her face. She was looking coyly over her shoulder, hair a-gleam beneath the arc-lamps, lustrous eyes and an inviting smile. On the back Toni had written 'Averil Day' and the date.

I hadn't known that she and Averil were acquainted, though of course with their stage connections I could see it was not impossible. I slipped it back in its place. I leant against the table.

'Gosh, I've got a head,' I said. 'Think I'll take a couple of aspirins and lie down for a while. I've been sleeping rottenly lately. As a matter of fact, I haven't had a decent night's sleep since Father died.'

'Poor kid, that's rotten,' said Toni with vague sympathy.

'I shall do something about it if it doesn't get better soon. Get some sleeping-stuff. I don't like those sort of things, I think they're dangerous, but it's simply idiotic to go on like this, isn't it? I suppose you don't happen to know of anything, good harmless stuff?'

'Not me. I always sleep like a top, thank God. Tell you what though. Curdie takes something. He sleeps badly; he's so highly strung, you know. Whatever he takes must be pretty harmless because he's been taking it for years, I believe, but I expect it's strong. He always says it takes the kick of a mule to get him to sleep, his brain is so active. I'll ask what it is. He won't recommend it unless it's safe for you to take.'

I had increased my knowledge by just this much: that Toni knew Averil Day personally and that Curdie Baxter used a hypnotic. I wondered if it was paraldehyde, but did not dare to ask in case she remembered the name as well as I did. I didn't care, I was quite satisfied with my little bit of detecting, as far as it went.

I had no need to tell my family anything about Rex because it was all in the evening papers, plastered across in screamers, with hideous old-fashioned photographs taken years ago. And the horrible cheap things they wrote about him! I only prayed they would not discover my name in connection with his. I had seen what reporters could do to you in the States.

Mother and Toni were suitably shocked. Olivia came over as soon as she read the news to condole with me very sweetly and sympathetically.

'Did you know that he was married?' I asked.

'Good heavens, no, my poor child. What made you think so?'

'Oh, I don't know. The way you were kind of warning me against him before.'

'No, it was sheer instinct. I didn't like the man. A case of Dr. Fell. I told your brother that I didn't trust him and that was why he stopped being so friendly with him. I wish now that I could have persuaded you too, darling.'

'Oh, well,' I shrugged, as if I didn't care

one way or another. 'Have you seen Terry lately?'

Olivia shook her head. 'I was going to ask you that. I hope he's all right.'

As if on a stage cue, the 'phone bell rang. I stretched a lazy arm over the back of the sofa and lifted the receiver to my ear. 'Hullo.'

'Hullo yourself. And how's little sister?' came Terry's voice.

He too offered his sympathy and wanted to know all about it. I told him no more than he could read in the papers for himself. He said he wished he could be with us but circumstances forced him to remain in Town for a few days. Was there anything he could do? I said, 'Nothing.'

'Who did it, Judy?'

'Gosh, I wish I knew. How's your arm, by the way?'

'Oh, it's all right. Damned inconvenient, that's all.'

'Would you like to speak to Olivia?'

'Not particularly. Is she there?'

'Yep. Hold the line one moment please. I handed the instrument across to her,

188

and strolled innocently out of the room. I wandered upstairs. There was something I wished to ask Millicent, and I drifted into her room. She was lying on the bed with her eyes closed, the telephone lying comfortably in the crook of her neck. I thought she must have gone to sleep like that. But when she heard me her heavy white lids flew back and she raised her finger quickly to her lips and then placed her hand over the mouth piece of the receiver. She raised her moth-wing eyebrows at me and mouthed, 'What is it?' and then, 'Wait a moment.'

I fidgeted unhappily. 'Mother, you can't,' I whispered ' . . . a private conversation . . . it's dreadful.'

Her misty eyes were listening, intent — but not on me. At last, she grimaced and smiled and replaced the receiver.

'I left Olivia alone so that she could say whatever she wanted to. But to eavesdrop . . . I really think that is quite disgusting of you, Mother,' I said sternly.

'Don't be a prig, my darling daughter. Anyone who talks secrets or is indiscreet over the 'phone deserves all they get.

Besides, it was a very interesting conversation, as it happened. Not particularly lovey-dovey, as you assumed, but full of meat.' She smiled at me secretively.

'Very likely.' Like Queen Victoria I was not amused. I felt to blame. I stood by Millicent's cluttered desk and pushed the papers about with my forefinger. 'How would you like it if I read your private papers, eh?'

'You're welcome to, infant, if you think it would divert you at all. Perhaps you could even make order out of chaos.'

But I wasn't listening to her. I was staring at a small piece of crumpled paper. It was upside down, and I was trying to decipher the characters. I made out the words, 'Suppose I tell the police what I know, Baby'; and then Millicent came up behind me and started moving the papers about. It wasn't in her writing, anyhow, that much I was sure of. I suggested that I help her gather the papers into bundles, at least, and docket and mark them. She said, Well, if I promised not to throw anything away, however trivial it appeared, because she had a habit of writing astrological notes on any scraps of paper that came to hand.

I went downstairs and contrived to get rid of Olivia fairly soon. Millicent was at the desk still when I returned. I began making neat piles of the papers according to their subject-matter. Millicent was right; on the backs of bills, the edges of letters, in the margins of her account-books were scribbled remarks about the planets and prophecies. But though I searched methodically and scanned both sides of every piece of paper, I did not come across the one I was looking for again. I did discover more stuff in the same writing, though, and I asked her if it was Neville's — quite casually — and she said it was. So I was that much wiser anyway.

When I had straightened the desk, I went out in search of Neville. As I walked across the fields I pondered the meaning of the brief message I had glimpsed. Heaven knew I did not wish to jump to conclusions, but I could not for the life of me see how it could possibly mean anything but what it said. But to whom was it addressed? 'Suppose I tell the police what I know, Baby.' Was that a mere suggestion or was it a warning, a hint of blackmail? I recalled only too well the conversation I had unwittingly overheard between my mother and Neville, the day I had so nearly drowned.

Neville was silhouetted poetically against the westering sun, leaning against the fence surrounding the sties. He was meditatively scratching the back of Matilda, our prize sow, with the end of his thick ash stick. I leant beside him.

'Let me do that. I've always wanted to,' I begged.

Obligingly he handed the stick across. I scraped it back and forth over Matilda's bristles, to the accompaniment of her grunts. Neville, I realized, had not seen the paper yet with the news of Rex's death in it.

'What have you been doing to yourself?' I asked. 'You've got blood on your pants.' And true enough there was a dark reddish-brown smear on the cuff of his trousers, but whether of blood or not . . .

'Have I?' he said vaguely. 'Where? Oh,

that, that's nothing. I'm always bashing myself about. Nearly cut my leg clean off the other day, trying to get the hang of how to use a swaphook.'

'Oh, that reminds me,' I said quickly. 'Does one have to have a licence for a gun over in this country, and are they difficult to get?'

'You do and they are. What do you want one for?'

'I want to do some target-practice.'

'Got to keep your eye in, eh? Are you one of them thar cow-girls who can drill a hole in the ace of spades at fifty paces and roll a cigarette in each hand? I can lend you a gun, if you promise not to hurt yourself with it,' he offered.

'Thanks a lot. I wanted a revolver actually. I suppose you don't happen to have such a thing on you?'

'I expect I can rootle my old service revolver out of somewhere for you. But don't you let anyone know, or there'll be a rumpus.'

I thanked him awfully and promised I'd be very careful.

'Well,' I said, and relinquished the

stick. 'Guess I'd better get back and change for dinner.'

'By Jove, yes,' he agreed, and fell into step beside me.

We walked in silence for a while, and then I thought it best to break the sad news to him. Otherwise he was going to think me completely callous. I gave him a digest of the evening papers.

'Poor little girl,' he said, and pulled at his ragged moustache. 'You are getting it raw, aren't you? I expect you feel pretty cut-up about it, don't you? You've got plenty of what it takes, I will say that,' he added sentimentally.

'You can't expect me to feel very heartbroken about someone who was playing me for a sucker, can you?'

'I suppose not.'

'You knew he was a bigamist, didn't you, Neville?'

'Why, no. What makes you say that, old girl?'

'Nonsense, of course you did. You weren't a bit surprised when I told you just now.'

'No, I wasn't surprised, I suppose. I

always suspicioned he was a wrong 'un. He'd been in quod, I knew that, but I didn't know what for. And it's not exactly the sort of thing one asks a chap, though I might have if I'd liked him.'

'Why, how did you know that?' I said admiringly.

'There are certain unmistakable signs to the discerning eye. Quod leaves its hallmark on you in the same way that a public-school does.'

'An old school tie that never fades.'

Exactly.'

I stared at him curiously. He caught my scrutiny, and laughed slightly.

'Oh, I don't mind, little girl. It was years ago and besides it was to shield someone. Just an innocent kid I was,' he sighed.

Gosh, I thought, isn't life perfectly *awful*. I wondered if there was really and truly anyone decent in the whole world, if one knew *all* about them.

'You won't broadcast it, old lady, all the same, will you? I wouldn't like your dear mother to know. She might not be as broadminded as you are about it. And you know it isn't easy to get a decent job nowadays, at my age. I've had some *nice* jobs, I can tell you, washing dishes in a filthy Greek restaurant once, and another time spying on the staff in a hotel to see they didn't steal — that sort of thing. Though it lowers one's prestige somewhat. I mean, when one considers that one is an Old Harringovian, after all.'

It dawned on me as I was changing later, that the sentence I read upside down might have been, 'Suppose I tell the police, what I know, BRADY.' After all, Neville was not an American, nor the sort of person to use the expression, Baby. I could not imagine him addressing Millicent so. Old lady was his favourite term. But BRADY, ah, that was different. He knew something about Rex. At the very least he knew he was an old lag. And suppose, oh God, suppose he knew — had found out somehow — that Rex was responsible for Elsie's death . . . Something, perhaps, that he was not able to prove, and so had taken the law into his own hands.

Not so fast, I told myself sternly. Why

should Rex have killed Elsie in the first instance? Perhaps he knew that Elsie Thompson was not me, and so he killed her to get her out of the way before I appeared. But that didn't make sense. Because why not just wait till I turned up and then confront the imposter with the real person? Then why should he want to kill someone who was masquerading as me? He had every reason to keep me alive and not to dispose of me, hadn't he? It was crazy. Unless — unless he did it simply and solely to scare me. Yes, that was it. I trembled with dread.

Either this Elsie was up to some little game of her own and Rex happened on her and saw it all in a flash. Or he had inveigled her down on some pretext or another and then killed her. And why? He had to be able to *prove* to me somehow, didn't he, that I was in danger of my life? And if my family were not really attacking me, then *he* would have to fake attacks on me. I could see that that would be dangerous; for either it might nearly come off, or it might — overbalancing in the direction of safety — appear so slight as to be coincidental. What better move could he make than to actually kill someone who might have been me. If that didn't convince me, nothing would.

To think I nearly married him, a murderer and a bigamist! Now what was I supposed to do about Neville. He'd rubbed out a rotter. But two wrongs did not make a right. But then I had no proof, really, unless you count a silly little bloodstain, plus the fact that he owned a revolver and knew a thing or two about Rex . . .

Terry's door was open and as I ran downstairs I poked my nose in, for no reason at all. It looked different, and I stared about me trying to figure out what it was. Then I got it. The revolver was no longer on top of the chest of drawers. I pulled open the drawers and rummaged inside hopefully. Lay down on my stomach and looked to see if it had slipped on to the floor. At last I gave up. It was not there. Who would have taken it? And why?

It left me with an uneasy feeling. I could not forget that it was loaded.

The next day the fun began in earnest. It was only to be expected, I knew, that the reporters should find out about me sooner or later. They were down on us bright and early next morning, like the Assyrians. They leapt out on one from every quarter, grinning with feigned politeness and sympathy.

Toni was perfectly wonderful with them, and gave them as good as she received. She wasn't cross or uncommunicative. On the contrary, she was positively verbose. But she refused to talk of anything but herself and Curdie's prospective theatre. She certainly knew how to utilise her opportunities. They printed quite a lot of the stuff for want of anything better.

10

The Police Make an Arrest

The papers said that the police expected to make an arrest soon. But we were inclined to think that was the usual propaganda and didn't really mean anything.

We were all deeply depressed anyway, especially me — with never a minute's peace from the reporters and the police. The Chief Constable used to come over from Garthurst and bark at us furiously, like an Airedale browbeating a tramp. And there was some talk about Scotland Yard being called in, which didn't cheer up anyone

There no longer seemed any privacy or peace for any of us. I hardly dared poke my nose outside the front door for fear it would be bitten off by curiosity-hunters.

Then Olivia, taking pity I suppose on our misery, drove up to town and brought back Terry to cheer us up. He looked well, though his hand was still in a splint.

He pretended to be very angry. What was the use of giving way?

If one could not get out, the thing was to have one's friends in. We must give a party. He outlined it energetically.

'Oh, darling, nothing ostentatious,' begged Millicent.

'Nonsense,' he declared. 'Stop cowering before them. You've got to show the world that none of this means anything to you. You never were mixed up with this bigamist; it's nothing to do with you at all. It's a libel to say otherwise. Have a party to clear the air. Nothing gaudy, you know, but perfectly natural . . . You need a man about the house. Can't think what Neville was up to, to let you get all morbid about it.'

He dispatched Toni and Olivia to Garthurst to get the eats while I was to help him collect the guests. I was to help him by dialing the automatic 'phone for him, which he protested was awkward for his left hand and impossible for his right. Really, I guessed, he wanted my company.

Millicent, he said, was to prophesy by stars, cards, crystal, or what-have-you whether the party would be a success or not.

'Shall we have a funny party or a crazy party?'

'What's the difference?' I wanted to know.

'Why, a funny party is one where you have all the sorts of friends who mix in well, so you have fun. And a crazy party is one where you ask all kinds of people who will loathe one another — like county and artistic, and then you go crazy. See?'

I betted it was going to be a difficult party whoever we had.

'Let us for a start rub out all the county people and all the vulgar people, and just have folks we like,' I said, ticking off names in the old address book.

But when he rang up the ones we had chosen, he admitted I was right. They were nearly all vulgar. He had a job to answer and parry their indiscreet questions about me and Rex. When the fourth person asked him who he supposed had murdered Rex, he said, 'Why don't you ring up the police and ask them? Why should you expect us to know?' and banged down the 'phone irritably.

'Aren't they *awful*? It'll be a very small party, but you won't mind that, will you?' he said.

'My dear, I expected it. Of course they want to know who did it. So do I. So do you, don't you?'

'Yes,' said Terry. 'Who did?'

'What about Mrs. Garnet? The way she came in just at that moment seems pretty fishy to me. A very curious coincidence.'

'A very unfortunate coincidence for her, though. Why on earth didn't she bunk away quick afterwards, before anyone spotted her? Unless . . . Would you say she was a clever woman, Judy?'

'Hard to say. She had that frumpish look so many clever people have. Why?'

'I was going to say; unless she was counting on no one believing that anyone who had committed a murder could behave quite so stupidly.'

'You've hit it in one, Terry.'

We rounded up a few more friends on the 'phone; and then we descended into the cellar to select the drinks. Seeing Toni's little photo gallery reminded me.

I said, 'Do you suppose it is difficult to get paraldehyde? Would one need a prescription, for instance?'

'Paraldehyde, what's that?'

And when I explained to him. 'I don't know, but I should hope so. Don't you start drugging yourself, my girl, or there'll be trouble. I'll take you out for a nice brisk walk before you go to bed tonight, and I'll guarantee you'll sleep all right.'

'Forget it,' I said. 'I wouldn't drug. I just wondered. Toni suggested it to me, that's all. Tell me, Terry, what do you think of Neville?' I swung up beside him on a wine bin.

'Oh, a good-hearted kind of rotter. Can't think what Millicent sees in him. But she's always attracted to these meretricious wasters.'

'Mmmm. Did you know — this is in confidence — that he had been to prison?'

'Really?' He didn't seem frightfully astonished. 'And Brady or Garnet, or whatever his name was. Quite a little colony of ex-lags round here. What was he in for?'

'He didn't tell me. He said it was when he was very young, to shield somebody else.'

'He would say that. Real Salvation Army mind that chap's got.'

'What do you think it was, then?'

'If I had thought about it — which I didn't — I would have taken Rex to be a confidence-trickster. Bigamy is only a confidence-trick on a large scale. And Neville — what can we say about Neville? How about a spot of forgery, something quiet and refined?'

'Hmm. I should say blackmail personally. You don't think Neville could do a murder?'

'Good God, no. Not on your life!'

'And how about Rex?'

'Rex might possibly kill if it was very safe and worth his while; but that, too, is very unlikely. Not his line.'

'Well, it so happens that I'm pretty sure they *both* of them killed.'

Terry looked at me for a long time in sad silence. 'All right, I'll buy it.'

'I believe Neville killed Rex. I think he had found out that Rex had killed his daughter, but very likely there was no way to prove it. At first he wanted to blackmail him, and then I suppose he realized that he couldn't very well go to the police with so little proof, so he decided to take the law into his own hands.'

'It's a sweetly-pretty story, dear, but I don't quite get the bit about Rex killing Neville's daughter, though.'

'She was Averil Day, don't you remember? He killed her to frighten me.'

I caught Terry's expression. I had forgotten that he did not even know that Elsie Thompson was pretending to be me. I explained it to him now; and how Rex had tried to persuade me that I was in mortal danger. And what better way could he prove it than by showing me that someone masquerading as me was killed, and it might have been me. I skimmed as lightly as I could over the question of who was supposed to want to kill me. But Terry was no fool, he knew who benefited by my death. He was quite pale by the time I had finished.

'My God,' he said. 'The blackguard, the dirty blackguard!' His eyes were darkly dilated with anger. 'Why on earth didn't you tell me before? Fancy going through all that alone! You're like Jane Eyre.'

We laughed.

Terry said, 'And making out it was your own family, that was the beastliest part of it, so that you had no one to turn to, no one to advise you, always on your guard. No wonder you were in a hurry to get married and get out of it all. How you must have loathed us!'

'Oh no. The trouble was that I thought you loathed me — because of the money. That was what I couldn't *bear*.'

'Well, I guess we all felt pretty mad about it at first. And I was all ready to loathe you. But the minute I walked into the dining-room that evening it all went. You were too sweet to hate, and that was the end of it.'

'Do you want a kiss for that testimonial? The beastly money doesn't mean a thing to me. If you want any, ask me for it. Let there be no talk of mine and thine betwixt us.'

'Dearest, I hate to spoil a beautiful moment with such sordid matters, but I would be eternally grateful if you could lend me a couple of hundred quid for a little while.'

'Lend! I'll be glad to make you a present of it.'

'I only want a loan of it. And I'll pay you back as soon as I am able . . . If all goes well that may be quite soon.'

'What are you up to?'

'Monkey tricks.' He laid his forefinger on his nose with a sly look. 'There may be an announcement soon . . . ' He rolled his eyes and jumped down from the bin. 'But hist . . . the fair Antonia. No more of this, and pray you silence keep.'

And indeed Olivia and Antonia came down into the cellar before I could say another word. Did he really intend to propose to Olivia? I hoped so. And would she say yes? I watched them now, a handsome couple, like something on the films, with Terry devouring her with his eyes.

Toni held a bottle of sherry to the light.

'Look at our brother, will you?' she muttered from the side of her mouth.

'Now load up, girls,' said Terry. 'I can't carry more than three bottles in my left hand.'

Laden, we left the cellar single file.

I was rather dreading the party, but when the time came I found I was unexpectedly enjoying myself. There were very few people and almost all of them known to me. There was an intimate secretive air about it that reminded me of the midnight feasts we had held at school. I rather wished I had asked Bob Stone to come. He would have enjoyed it; and I would have liked to see him again. I was surprised and a little bit hurt that he had never written to me again. Surely he must have seen the papers? Probably, Bob had got over his feeling for me by now. Did I care? I decided that what I needed was another drink. I took one, and felt better.

Someone was playing the gramophone. In the dim, paneled hall Millicent and Neville were dancing very rapidly. Suddenly everyone was whirling round and round to a Viennese waltz. Curdie appeared from nowhere and swept me into his arms, jogging round with me rapidly. No one heard the bell ring above the music. None of them, rapt in their own twirling orbits, noticed Lucy, the little maid, slip through the dancers and open the hall door. But then, unmistakably, everyone faltered to a standstill, and the soundbox grated noisily across the disc, pushed by a careless hand to silence.

We remained frozen into unexpected immobility as Babyface came ponderously across the parquet floor. I felt sick with apprehension.

He stood in the middle of the floor and apologised for interrupting us. He looked round the room and then he came across to me. Curdie's arms dropped away from me.

Babyface said, 'Miss Judith Allen? I have here a warrant for your arrest for the murder of Graham Garnet alias Rex Brady.'

Terry sprang forward. 'You're mad! You can't do that!'

Babyface put his hand on Terry's chest.

'You mustn't obstruct me in the performance of my duty, sir,' he said solemnly.

Terry thrust out his splinted arm impulsively, and then let it drop to his side.

Everyone was looking horribly uncomfortable. 'Of course, there is some mistake,' they were muttering soothingly to one another.

I began to laugh, deep shaking laughter from the pit of my stomach.

'And I have to warn you that anything you say will be taken down and may be used in evidence,' said Babyface stolidly. 'Now, Miss, if you are ready . . . ' He put his hand on my arm, gripping my wrist with a deadly snap of finality. That brought it home to me as though cold steel gripped my heart. My laughter stopped as if it had been cut with a knife. I could have died of fear just then. Blackness whirled about me, and I thought with horror that I was going to faint . . .

'I can't bear it — I can't *bear* it — ' Millicent's voice came hoarsely, as though it was being torn out of her alive. Neville was leading her away.

'It's all right, little 'un,' called Toni. 'It's a mistake. It must be. I'll get on to the Chief Constable right away.'

They watched me go. The light from the doorway illumined the steps with a zigzagging square of gold. All the way down to the police-car I was desperately trying to wake myself up from the nightmare . . . I was at the car without having made any conscious effort to walk there. I was in the car, and the door shut behind me; and still I was not awake. The car slid away into the darkness, bearing me with it, into a night that was to show no glimpse of dawn for me for a long time to come . . .

PART TWO

PART TWO

11

Robert Stone Steps In

When I opened my morning paper and saw that Judy had been arrested for the murder of Rex Brady, I didn't even stop to finish my breakfast. The girl I was nuts about had just been presented with a lovely steel bracelet by the Government. I chucked a toothbrush into my grip and beat it for the jalopy.

I'd rather been expecting something to break. The set-up hadn't appealed to me from the start. I had hated leaving her alone down there among what seemed to me a gang of crooks. And as for Brady! Of course I had no idea what his little game was then, but I didn't like the look of him; he had that suave, dago look that women always fall for. Well, I had had my congé from him right enough, so I didn't go back to see how she was getting on. Besides, she knew my address if she felt like contacting me. I'm glad I didn't know she got herself engaged to that sly spider till afterwards — or, or *I* might have been his murderer.

I was surprised to read that he had been found shot in a hut on Breem Hill. However, that made me keep my eyes skinned for further developments. When they materialised, I wished with all my heart they hadn't.

Not that it occurred to me even for one moment that Judy might have shot him. I knew that was a hateful mistake. The idea of Judy behind bars, even for twenty-four hours, was nauseating.

The poor old jalopy nearly bust her guts trying to make it as fast as I wanted to; but between us we did it, and pulled up in scorching triumph outside the police station a couple of hours later.

They wouldn't tell me anything at first. Then I wormed out of them that she wasn't being detained there at all, but had been taken over to Garthurst.

'Well, can you give me a permit?' I asked. 'It's important that I see her.'

Sorrowfully they had to refuse. The

Chief Constable, they intimated discreetly, might be persuaded to give me one.

'Yep, I know. In three weeks' time, after he's found out all about me. That won't do for Bob Stone, gentlemen. Give me the address of her lawyer?'

They did not know the address of Miss Allen's lawyer. They were not aware that anyone had been entrusted with the defence as yet.

'You dirty rats,' I said. 'I bet you never even told her she was entitled to it.' And I was out of there and half-way to Garthurst before they had could impugn me for slander.

I strode furiously into the Garthurst police station and demanded to be directed to the Chief Constable immediately.

It seemed he was distracting his sadly burdened mind with a game of golf at a course some five miles away.

'That's too bad,' I said. 'I guess you'll just have to pass me in, anyway, without waiting for his official say-so. I have to see Miss Allen, the prisoner in the Garnet case.'

'I'm afraid you can't see the prisoner without a permit,' said the damned policeman deferentially.

I said, 'Listen, you have a young girl in there who's scared stiff. No one has had the decency to get her a lawyer or anything. I can't do very much harm if I see her for just five minutes. I only want to tell her that she isn't alone, that I'm working to get her out of there.'

'I'd let you through if I could, sir, but it's against regulations. As for the young lady's defence, I dare say her family will see to that.'

'That's what *you* think. All right. I only hope that your Chief Constable is good and mad at you for letting me interrupt his game.'

Back into the jalopy once more and off at top speed to the golf course, and then hurrying over the rough in search of my victim. He swung his niblick ferociously at me when I explained my errand. He ignored my credentials, and refused to hear my arguments, maintaining that he was not to be browbeaten by any blasted Yankee. So I admitted despairingly that I loved her. He coughed irritably and begged me to leave him alone, he wasn't concerned with my damned emotions. He borrowed a leaf from my notebook and scrawled an authorisation on it for me.

'There you are. You can see the wretched girl for twenty minutes. And now kindly go away.'

And I did.

Back in Garthurst I handed them the paper and the policeman took me along to Judy. She was sitting meekly, her hands in her lap, staring in front of her. She was pale, and her eyes didn't light up when I came in; back of them there lurked a horrid sort of beaten look.

I said, 'Hiya, babe!'

She didn't answer. Instead, her chin quivered helplessly and the tears spilled over the fringe of her lashes and down her cheeks.

I stuck my fist under her chin gently and said, 'Come on, darling, you don't want to throw in the towel in the first round. Be a big girl.'

She said, 'Oh, Bob, I was so scared you wouldn't come. But I knew you would.

How am I going to get out of here?'

'Well, I'm glad you were waiting for me,' I said. 'We'll have you walking out of this door in no time,' I prophesied.

'You don't think they'll hang me, do you?' she whispered.

'Hang you!' I scoffed. 'They don't hang innocent people in this country.'

'I know,' she said softly. 'But I guess they don't arrest them, either, unless they have pretty good proof.'

'What proof have they got?'

'That's what scares me. They must have something more than I know about.'

I persuaded her to tell me as much as she knew about herself. It was a fact that things didn't look exactly rosy. We needed to find out just what they had against her. Meanwhile she had to guard herself carefully. And I promised to locate a real up-and-up lawyer to prevent the other side scoring goals at her expense.

Time was up. But I promised to come again as soon as I could. She looked a lot better when I left her, and she thanked me for coming.

The first place for me was her home, I

decided, heading the jalopy for Elder Hall, before bothering with a lawyer or anything else. I absolutely had to get the lay-out up there.

It had a subdued, disheveled air somehow, I thought to myself as I stood in the hall and waited for the maid to come back to tell me Mrs. Allen couldn't see me. But to my surprise she conducted me right along to her, after explaining that Mrs. Allen was resting and would see me in her room. And then the door opened and I saw an immense, pale woman shimmer towards me in a flutter of veils.

Her outstretched hands clasped mine.

'Oh, Mr. Stone, do please forgive me for receiving you like this, but I am absolutely *distracted*. Do sit down . . . I feel I know you quite well, because my little girl — ' her voice broke and she looked away from me, her big shoulders heaving. 'It's so awful. If only I could think of something to do . . . It's at times like these that a woman feels the need of a man so terribly.'

'That's why I'm here, Mrs. Allen, to

help you all I can,' I said. 'As much as you'll let me.'

'What shall we do, Mr. Stone? Or may I call you Bob? What do you advise?'

'Seemed to me the first thing to do was to contact a lawyer.'

'Yes, that was what my son Terry said. He's gone up to town to arrange about it now. And Antonia, my daughter, has a friend who is some kind of a big-wig in the Home Office, and she's gone to try and get him to do something, to get her released on bail or something. That is, if Toni can make an appointment with him.'

Rats deserting the ship, I thought. Why go all the way to town for a lawyer? What was wrong with the family lawyer, wherever he hung out? I suggested as much to her.

'Terry said he'd be no use at all in a case like this. Terry says this needs someone who handles murder cases as a general thing.'

I tried to persuade her that the very last thing we wanted was a display of publicity. This was not a case that called for sharp-dealing crook lawyers, used to dealing with criminals, and having a reputation for that. There were numerous advantages, too, in dealing with a local man, known to and respected by the local police. We needed someone quiet and steadfast, someone who knew every detail of the family history for generations back.

I hammered at her until I won my point and she consented. Reluctantly she gave me his address, muttering to herself that Terry was going to be furious with her. I reminded her that we had to consider Judy's welfare and not Terry's.

'You're quite right, Bob. I'm only so glad that my little Judy has got such a good friend. Tell me, I suppose you'll be staying down here for a while, where do you intend to put up?'

She was most insistent that I should not board at the local hostelry but should make my temporary home there with them. It had its advantages so I concurred. That way, I could keep an eye on them all. I stood up to leave.

'By the way,' I said, 'I am right in thinking that this is the second murder Judy has been tied up in, aren't I? Wasn't there a young girl? The day Judy arrived. The daughter of your bailiff, I believe.'

I watched her eyes widen and then the pale eyebrows frown down like silky moths. She gazed out of the window at the distant hill. 'His daughter,' she murmured. 'And now mine . . . I hadn't thought of that . . . ' She gave a tiny laugh, and held out her hand to me; and as she did so, fragments of torn lace and lawn fluttered to the floor.

I resolved that I must take a peek at this bailiff some time, but not now. The first thing to do now was to find that old lawyer and get him moving.

Once I had found the quiet old square tucked away behind the heart of the town he was easy to find. The solicitor's office was in a dignified eighteenth-century house that was practically unchanged. I guessed the air in the office was unchanged since those days too. I sent in my card and waited.

At length the prim little junior clerk ushered me into the dimly lit room with its leaded panes. The solicitor was so dried-up that he positively rustled. But I noticed that his eyes were alert and pricking like needles behind his pince-nez. He bade me good morning and offered me a chair.

'I understand that you are,' he consulted the card in his hand again, 'Mr. Stone, a representative of the Fidias Detective Agency in New York City?'

I signified that was correct, and he begged me to tell him how he might help me. I told him that I came in connection with the Allen-Brady case, mention of which had been made in the newspapers that morning,

'I have come on behalf of the family,' I said. 'They want your advice and aid.'

He seemed to think the family should have applied to him directly and not through an intermediary. Was I authorised by the family? By Miss Judith Allen?

'Look here,' I said, 'they none of them know who I am, not even Miss Judith. I've persuaded them to let me help them over this, but they don't know anything about me. It's an advantage for me to be working with a screen, and I don't want to drop it till I need. How I came into it at all was like this:

'About ten days after old man Allen died, the Fidias office received a confidential cable from this country demanding that a reliable agent be detailed to look after Miss Judith Allen, without her knowledge, day and night. It didn't say what she was to be guarded from, but guarded she was to be until she arrived safely at her destination, which was Elder Hall in England. That sounded a perfectly straightforward commission, and they put me on to it because I happened to be the agent nearest her own age, so that it would be easy for me to be with her pretty constantly without it seeming odd.

'I kept my eyes well-skinned all the time but I saw nothing suspicious. I figured that someone in her family didn't like the idea of such a young and pretty girl going around loose, and at the same time they didn't want to offend her by giving her a nanny. That was all right by me; I enjoyed the trip over. And I delivered her safely to her front door — or practically. Actually, I made a mistake in not going just that step farther with her, because that was when the fun began..

'Well, I came down a couple of days later to report to my employer and also see if Miss Allen was all right. They were together, and she introduced me. We both received a bit of a shock. He was very annoyed to find that I was so young to take such a responsible job. But I think it was more than that. I noticed that he didn't even know Judith as well as I did, and I didn't like the way he looked at her. I didn't know what his game was, but that there was some game I was sure. Still, my job was over and he dismissed me. I came back to Town, where I did some rummaging around and raked up quite a lot of dirt one way and another. There didn't seem much doubt that this Brady was a thorough rotter who was after Judith for her money. He had the forethought to hire someone to look after her from the word go and see she wasn't nabbed by some other blackguard. Then I traced back that he was a professional whose real name was Garnet, and that had me scared cold, because it looked to me when I saw them together that Judith had been more than a little impressed by the snake. Before I had time to warn her or do anything further, I learnt that he had been killed. Well, I didn't shed any tears over that. And I waited hopefully for a message from Judy which didn't come . . . and then I read, this morning, that she had been arrested. Something had to be done about that right away; and I came down to do it. That's the lot,' I concluded. 'Thank you for listening so patiently. And I do hope that you feel we can work together on this.'

'It's a most unsavoury case,' he said distastefully.

'Well, if it strikes you as unsavoury, what do you suppose it seems to a young girl?'

'Young man, you're in love with her, and that is all there is to it.'

'When you see her, sir, you'll fall in love with her yourself.'

He chuckled. 'We'll see, we'll see . . . And now let us get down to business. What is it all about?'

I told him as much as I knew. Now and

again he made a brief hieroglyphic on the pad beside him. When I had finished, he leant back and announced that he was going down to the Garthurst police station immediately. There was much to be done and little time in which to do it.

'And how can I learn the results, sir?'

'By coming to dine with me tonight,' he said briefly, and turned away, calling to his clerk to do half a dozen things at once.

12

Family History

I was acutely aware that I had had no breakfast by the time I got back to Elder Hall. Mrs. Allen smiled approvingly and said that she liked to see a healthy appetite, so I tucked in without feeling bashful. Antonia rang up and I gathered she had not been entirely successful with her Home Office big-wig. She reported crossly that she was coming home.

'All right, darling,' said Mrs. Allen soothingly, adding: 'Toni, do you know where Terry is . . . ? Oh, well, tell him not to bother, dear. Tell him that a friend of Judy's has fixed up everything here . . . Yes, he's here staying with us . . . Right beside me. Would you like to say Hullo . . . ? Well, I'll give him your love and say you look forward to seeing him later, is that it . . . ? And don't forget my message, lovey. Bye-bye.'

Replacing the phone, she turned to me. 'You haven't told me yet what old Gruff-and-grim had to say.'

'Not much. He listened, while I outlined the case to him. But I'm dining with him tonight, and I dare say he'll have something to tell me then.'

'But he was hopeful on the whole?'

'He never expressed an opinion. But don't let that depress you, Mrs. Allen, He deals in hard facts, and facts tend to keep you off snap judgments.'

'I *hope* we've done the right thing . . . Have a little more pie, dear boy.'

Then somehow we were on her pet subject and in no time at all we were whirling away among remoter universes, led and entangled by spirit-guides with odd names.

'My dear boy, I simply *must* do your horoscope. Come with me a minute.' She led me into her room, where I had first seen her, and began scuffling among the papers on her desk, dropping a trail of papers behind her. I knelt down and began massing them together, pausing to stare at the curious drawings. On the reverse side of one, roughly depicting sun, moon, and earth, with lines drawn between them intersecting the signs of the zodiac, was written a message that began: 'Judy, darling . . . ' and was signed, 'Rex Brady.' I didn't stop to read it then but, with a quick glance up at Mrs. Allen to see she was not looking, I stuffed it into my pocket. She found what she was looking for and began to explain it to me laboriously. I cut through the heart of her inconsequential chatter.

'Mrs. Allen, who do *you* think killed Rex Brady?'

She clasped her cheeks in both hands. 'I don't know,' she whispered. 'I'm afraid to think . . . '

'Afraid to think,' I said bitingly. 'Consider what you are saying, Mrs. Allen. You know that someone could have done it, someone might have done it, and you are afraid because that person means more to you than your own daughter, and you would rather sacrifice Judy than risk a show-down. What kind of a woman are you?'

'Please don't attempt to use your

vulgar third-degree methods on me,' she said coldly. 'We don't care for that sort of thing over here, particularly from our *guests.*'

I rubbed my forehead and apologised. It was a momentary craziness, I said, because I was so fond of Judy and so anxious about her. I was at a disadvantage because I did not know the people involved in this business. Therefore I needed to pick up all I could about them. Any information, anyone's impressions, were so much grist to the mill. In any case, hiding knowledge or even suspicion was worse than useless in the long run, and slowed but could not arrest the wheels of justice . . . And more slop from the same pail. But she seemed to take it all right.

'You misunderstood me, Bob. Of course, I'll tell you all I know. Don't you think I'm longing to have my little baby free again . . . ?'

'And poor Major Thompson, too. Or do you think the two murders are unconnected?'

'I can't think why Neville's poor little

girl should have been murdered.'

'She was a bait. A decoy duck, Mrs. Allen. Of no importance at all. That is, if the two murders are connected.'

'Oh, don't you think one of that horrid man's wives might have had their revenge on him? I can't honestly see why anyone should bother otherwise.'

'Can't you, Mrs. Allen? And yet you had very good reason to wish him well out of the way. For once Judy was married to him, the money she inherited passed out of the Allens' hands for good and all. Oh yes, Mr. Brady was a very inconvenient feature of the landscape. Yet, you know, he must have realized his danger once Judy told him that she had confessed her great secret to you all. That was why he was so insistent that it *should* be kept a secret that was why it was to be an elopement. So leaving all else aside, it suited your family, Mrs. Allen, for Brady to be liquidated just then.'

She said slowly, 'But do you really imagine that any of us would kill another human being for *money?* Why, it simply doesn't mean enough, it isn't all that important, can't you see?'

'And yet it has been done, if not in this instance in many others.'

'Well, lord knows, I need money — desperately, but I can't imagine that that could ever arouse me to murder. Hatred. Revenge. Passion. I can understand the lust for killing there. But mere gain . . . ' She shrugged. 'I suppose if I'd ever given it a moment's thought I would have realized that my husband was unlikely to leave his money to us. Too late to bother about it now, at all events.'

Mrs. Allen was one of those maddeningly subtle fools. I would talk with her again when I had more leisure, I thought. At present, I wished to locate Major Thompson and see what he had to give me. On my way down I had a stroke of luck; a letter for Terence was on the hall-table, readdressed and waiting to be reposted. I made a note of the address. I needed to see him and I meant to run up to Town and have a chat with him. If he happened to be on his way back here when I called — well, that would have its compensations too.

That was my second bit of luck, for finding the note from Rex to Judy, the missing note inviting her to come to the hut, was pure velvet. Now that I was unobserved I took another look at it. The writing was the same as in the two letters I had received at his hand when I was employed by him. When I got back to Town I would compare it with an actual specimen though.

Strolling across a field where cows grazed peaceably I came on Thompson, recognising him from the description. 'I'm not trespassing,' I called. I explained that I was a visitor at Elder Hall, and started chatting affable nonsense. He obligingly pointed out various landmarks about the countryside.

'That's Breem Hill,' he said.

'Where that man was murdered last week . . . ? Why, that's quite a thrill, isn't it . . . ? What a pity you weren't standing just here when it happened, you'd likely have seen the murderer going up or coming down.'

'Oh, they didn't go up this side, whoever they were. Anyone on that kind of errand would have tried to keep his coming and going a secret and not have used a public pathway in full view of any labourers on the estate.'

'Oh, I see. For a moment I thought you meant you *had* been here then and had *not* seen anyone.'

He thought for a moment. 'No, I wasn't here that day.'

'Hard lines . . . Did you know the chap personally?'

'Only very slightly.'

'What kind of a chap was he? The papers say he was a bigamist.'

'I didn't cotton to him. He wasn't quite — out of the top drawer, shall we say?'

I nodded. 'One can't help feeling that a chap must be a bit of a rotter to get himself murdered.'

Thompson suddenly snuffled, and shook his head.

'My girlie, my little Elsie — ' he broke off, his eyes watering. 'As good and sweet as you make 'em, she was, and clever too. Making a real name for herself . . . And then she was murdered . . . by some dirty bastard . . . And if I ever get my hands on him — or her . . . '

I sympathised. How was it the police had not yet tracked the criminal down? How slack they were over here. Hadn't he anything to work on, himself?

Sure, he had a pretty shrewd idea who had done it, and their motive. No, he couldn't tell the police because as yet it was no more than a suspicion. He preferred to work alone, and then when the whole thing was sprung he would present it to the police. They could have the glory of it; he would be satisfied with justice and retribution. He was advancing steadily nearer the goal. He knew something more now. For he was almost positive that the two crimes were committed by the same person. And for the same reason.

'But you must tell the police. If he's already killed two people, who knows when he may strike again? It is your duty, sir, to speak to the police.'

'In theory, yes,' he said irritably. 'In practice it comes out a different colour. I'm not talking. Besides,' he rubbed his jaw, 'it may be more advantageous to me to make my own terms over this, and not to speak at all . . . Everyone, they say, has his or her price. Why shouldn't it be true?'

'Is your price high?' I asked, as if I was joking.

'No. Very reasonable . . . considering.'

'I don't want to teach you how to suck eggs, sir, but there is a risk attached to that kind of revenge, unless one has really damning evidence. It so often happens that the criminal applies for police protection, pretending that he is being blackmailed. And then the balloon goes up — with no one inside. Horrid word, blackmail, isn't it . . . ? Of course, it depends a lot on the psychology of the criminal . . . In the ordinary way it may be a risk worth taking, but if the crime has been for mercenary motives . . . people will do everything they can in order to protect their ill-gotten gains,' I sighed.

But he was not listening. He was stroking one of the cows, examining her udders. Apparently, he had not heard a word of what I was saying.

'Well,' I said. 'Guess I'd better be going. Thanks for the talk.' I went a little way and then I turned round. 'Another thing,' I said, 'if you do know anything, whatever it is, you're in danger until you've passed on that knowledge. Actual personal bodily danger. The criminal would need to get you out of his way as much as anyone.' I walked away and left him staring at me over the cow's head.

Mr. Lockett, the solicitor, was waiting for me in his hideous but cosy little Victorian study. He held a decanter to the light.

'Bristol Cream,' he said, handing me a shallow glass full of tawny sherry. 'Your health, sir!'

I sipped it appreciatively as I waited for him to broach the all-important subject.

A maid announced that dinner was served.

He gave me sideways glance. 'Before we go in I had better tell you that I never discuss business during meals.'

And the beastly, selfish, old man led the way into a prim dining-room. We put on our nosebags and got down to it, with desultory remarks about current prices and the possible result of the year's harvest . . .

Eventually the meal was over, and we retired to the study again for coffee.

'Now, then,' I said. 'For goodness sake, let's have it.'

He clipped the end of a cigar with precision before replying.

'She's a darling. Pretty as paint, and courageous. Even if I didn't like you, young man, I'd help her out of this unholy mess. But she doesn't know, fortunately, just how bad her position is . . . I had a little chat with the constabulary . . . '

He held the match steady so that the flame licked the end of the cigar to a glowing crimson circle.

'The main thing is this. The bullet that killed Brady, or Garnet, came from a Colt .38. They have found the gun itself, or so they claim. It is a licenced revolver in Terence Allen's name, and it was found in his room. It was loaded, but one shot had been fired from it. When they examined it for fingerprints, amongst a few blurred ones, those of Judith Allen's stood out unequivocally — on the butt, on the trigger, everywhere. But that is circumstantial evidence.'

'You don't think it's true, do you?'

'One simply has to take these things into account and examine them at all points microscopically, in order to determine the value of the evidence. The police would have been chary of arresting a young girl of Miss Allen's standing unless the circumstantial evidence was very strong. Moreover, when I questioned her privately on these points she admitted that she had had the gun in her possession on the fatal day; but she swore that she had not had occasion to use it because he was already dead when she arrived. She had gone suspecting a trap and she had deemed it wise to protect herself with a gun — though whether she would have used it had the occasion arisen, she was not able to inform me. She maintains very stoutly that she had no inkling that he was a bigamist until his wife told her the next day. I only wish there was a little more substantial support to her story than faith.'

'I can provide one thread of support, anyway.' I rummaged in my wallet and produced the note from Rex that I had found on Mrs. Allen's desk. 'Here is the note she lost, that decoyed her to the hut. I know Brady's writing and it certainly seems to have been his. But we might use one of your specialists on it, on the off-chance. Anyway, it was a guileless assignation on her part.'

'That's immensely interesting.' He scrutinised it carefully through a pocket-magnifier. 'I'm afraid. I can't see clearly enough to judge. No matter, it shall be tested. Tell me, where did you come across it?'

'In Mrs. Allen's desk, or more accurately, on the floor, but *from* her desk. If you turn it over you'll see she has scribbled all over it. Now, why would she do that, do you suppose? If she had some good reason for taking it away from Judith, wasn't it very careless of her not to have destroyed it or put it in some safe place?'

'Millicent Allen is a very casual woman,' grunted Mr. Lockett. 'It's regarded as part of her charm. Can't stand sloppiness myself, but she is a good-natured creature, I'll say that for her. Well, it drove Frederick Allen to drink the way she went on, for he was of a precise and methodical style like myself. He had to put a notice in the paper at one time, I well remember, repudiating all responsibility for his wife's debts. Now, he couldn't bear advertisement in any form, and it riled him. And she didn't mend her ways either, and the children he found were being brought up to be as slack as she was. He believed in a fairly rigid training for the young, with emphasis on moral discipline. Poor old Frederick, I knew him well. People thought him a bit stiff and cranky, but it was only to balance his wife's wildness and extravagance. They were both nice creatures in their own way but they didn't happen to eat well out of the same plate. Well, Terence was grown-up and being rather trouble-some one way and another — there was a little matter of a cheque, I remember; and Antonia though only about fifteen was already setting out stubbornly on her own road to heaven or to hell, and Millicent was getting sloppier every day. From his point of view it just didn't seem worthwhile to go on. The breaking-point had been reached and he quietly made up his mind. He made her a generous allowance and agreed that she should keep on his beloved Elder Hall together with the estate and property, and he went away, taking with him his youngest and as yet fairly unspoilt child, Judith. And that was that. I was astonished when I heard that he had settled in America — of all places! — with his girl. The years passed and I forgot all about him, except as a remote client. Then came his unexpected death — and his even more unexpected will . . . If he could have foreseen all this!' Mr. Lockett shook his head gloomily.

'And do you consider that he was quite fair to his family? Was he too hard on them, do you think?'

Mr. Lockett pulled at his cigar. 'I told you that Frederick Allen and I had much the same character. I might have done the same in his position. I think they're a pretty scruffy lot, nice enough acquaintances, but bad friends. Careless, self-centred, and loose-moraled, I'd call them. I think he gave them a fair run for their money before he came to the conclusion that they were too black to be white-washed successfully.'

'As bad as that. Murderers, do you think?'

'That's what we have to find out.'

'What about the bailiff? He's a bad lot, isn't he? Been to jail, they say.'

'They say correctly. In 1927, for running an illegal gaming-establishment. There was some talk of a profitable sideline in the white-slave traffic, but they were never able to prove anything.'

'Then why should we suppose that he would stop short of murder?' I said.

'Only one reason that I know of. He's a lazy blighter. If he could get someone else to do the dirty work for him, he would.'

'Perhaps,' I mused aloud, 'his daughter was to pull the chestnuts out of the fire for him, but something misfired. Or else — But a little while ago he was telling me that he had a shrewd suspicion who the murderer was, and as good as admitted that he intended to blackmail him — or her . . . I had the feeling he really did suspect someone, and that that someone was — Mrs. Allen.'

Mr. Lockett's hands rustled as he rubbed them together. 'Isn't that very, very interesting? There has been quite a lot of gossip about the gallant Major and the beautiful Mrs. A. How interesting!' He shot me a sharp glance. 'Who killed Elsie Thompson? What reason had she to be killed except as Judith Allen? Who stood to gain by Elsie Thompson's death? Who killed Rex Brady? And how was it that he was killed with Terence's gun? How many people could have known about that gun? Was it mere accident that it bore Judith's fingerprints?'

I groaned. 'It makes me feel sick to my stomach.'

'Mind you, I am not saying that it is a member of the family, or at least they may be only indirectly responsible. There are outside people who have an equal interest in getting their claws on that money. Yes. One has to consider *every* possibility.'

'You are quite right, sir. I promised myself a little trip up to Town to squint into Terence's 'toon hoose,' and I'll have a look at that Curdie Baxter's private life at the same time. It might prove fruitful.'

He nodded affably. I felt we had covered a lot of useful ground. I got up and thanked him and said good-night.

13

Marriage of True Minds?

When I returned, Mrs. Allen and Major Thompson were in the library playing cribbage, like a contented old married couple. A deceptive appearance, each suspecting the other of knowing more about this dirty business than they let on.

A dark, slender girl with a sulky face was sprawling deeply in an armchair under a standard lamp with an open book in her hands. Mrs. Allen introduced her to me casually as her daughter, Toni. She acknowledged my greeting with a nod of the head. Mrs. Allen returned to her game. I stood there awkwardly, wondering whether to sit down or to go to bed. I was conscious that Toni had not turned a page for a long while; I could feel her eyes scrutinising me shamelessly.

' . . . One for his nob . . . ' cried Mrs. Allen. 'Toni, you're very unsociable this evening. You might try to entertain our guest.'

'I was just wondering what the hell he was doing, mixed up in our affairs.'

'Why, Toni, what a way to talk!' reproved her mother.

'I hope you don't think I'm interfering, Miss Allen?' I said.

'There are some kinds of trouble where you don't want outsiders poking in, however well-intentioned.'

'There is nothing to feel ashamed about, Miss Allen. Or frightened,' I added.

She laughed mirthlessly. 'I'm not *afraid* of you. It's mother . . . She has no sense of what is fitting, will let people walk all over her and do just as they please. She lets you — a complete stranger — walk in here and order her about, cancel our plans, rearrange the whole show, and she doesn't know a damn thing about you. But it's not good enough now. There's too much at stake.'

'My dear Toni,' interrupted Mrs. Allen, 'do give me credit for a little sense. If the lad is crooked, I'd far rather have him under my eye than roaming about in the dark waiting to stab me in the back at the first opportunity . . . And two for his heels!' she interpolated.

'Oh, well, there is nothing to be gained by prolonging this discussion,' said Toni, shrugging, and picking up her book again.

'Then, you don't mean to give me any assistance in my efforts to release your sister?'

She smiled sardonically and made no answer.

I strolled to the door. 'How come you never told the police you knew Averil Day?' I said.

'They never asked me — if it's any business of yours. Why should they?'

Thompson swung round to stare at her. '*I* never knew you knew Elsie,' he said.

'I didn't know her. I had *met* her. And you did know, because I told you. I gave her a complimentary sitting.'

'You never told me,' Thompson declared.

'All right,' she said languidly. 'What of it?'

'Now, Toni,' said her mother warningly.

The bailiff's eyes swung suspiciously from one woman to the other. You could see his thoughts ticking anxiously behind his dull eyes. What did it mean? Was any woman to be trusted? What were they driving at?

Having made my point, I was satisfied with my reward. Smiling, I retired to bed.

I was up early next morning for there was a lot to be done.

As I backed the jalopy out of the garage, I remembered Averil Day, and frowned as I tried to figure out just how that bit of business had been worked. Suppose it had been worked by Brady, for instance . . . ? One thing I would have to do, I reminded myself, was to have a little confidential chat with the owner of the car. *Where* she had lost it might prove an indication of who had taken it. Miss Fane, I noted, but that could wait till I returned.

I pulled up at my hotel first. There was no important mail for me, except a letter from the Fidias Agency ordering me to sail at the end of the week in order to report for duty on the following Friday to take over a big case. My God, I thought, I've *got* to clean up the whole business in less than a week. And if I don't? Do I sail and leave Judith in jail and waiting to be hanged? No damned fear! Let them fire me if they felt that way about it. There were other jobs. I tore the letter into fragments. Then I felt better.

I found Rex Brady's correspondence to me neatly filed away, and compared it with the note addressed to Judy. They appeared to have been written by the same hand. They were written on the same kind of cheap stationery. Now, I am no calligraphic expert, but under the magnifying-glass I thought I could discern certain irregularities. There were marks of hesitancy here and there in the middle of a letter; some of the upstrokes were rather thicker than they should have been, as though they had been *drawn upside down*. One thing I knew: forgers do not attempt to copy writing by imitating it as writing, but they turn the script upside down so that it no longer has any significance as letters for them and then they *draw* it, as they would a design. This method gives a more exact reproduction, but in unpractised hands it is inclined to leave betraying signs. If I was right, an expert would have no difficulty with it. Judy was as good as freed.

Terence Allen's little foot-on-the-ground was in a street of narrow houses which combined a rather dashing bohemianism with an air of gentility.

A scrag-end of a woman with a lively eye and a gap-toothed smile opened the door to me. I inquired for Mr. Allen.

'There now, he's gorn agine. You never seem to catch 'im, do yer?' She peered at me. 'Oh, aren't you the chap wot called twice last week? Oh, I'm ever so sorry, sir. Still there's no 'arm in being cautious. Thought you was the man come about the pianna Mr. Allen's got on the never-never.'

'Do you mean he is in really?'

She shook her head. 'An' I don't know when he'll be back, neither.'

'Oh dear,' I said. 'Here have I come all the way from America, not having seen

Terence since we were at school together, and — '

'You don't mean to say you come all the way from America just to see Mr. Allen,' she gasped.

'No, I don't,' I laughed. 'But I'm not here for long, and I did want to see him before I went back.'

'Lor, ain't you unlucky, sir . . . I could let you 'ave 'is 'ome address, if you like. Very likely you'd find him there.'

'No, I've just come from Elder Hall. I naturally went there first.'

That seemed to reassure her canny cockney heart. So I ventured to suggest lightly that I would like to write a note and leave it for him. Would she show me to his room? She would and did.

She led me upstairs to his two rooms, a bedroom and a sitting-room. She poked around for paper and ink in a familiar sort of way, as though the drawers held no mystery for her, gossiping divertingly enough the while. It was clear she had a soft spot for Terry, he was one of her young men, as she called her lodgers. I queried her about his reaction to the crime at Breem Hill. Yes, he felt pretty bad about it, that chap being a pal of his. And the very day it 'appened he'd been sitting 'ere laughing away as merry as anything with 'is girl friend, in spite of his broke wrist. Yes, proper cut up he was, when he heard about it.

The landlady hadn't heard yet that it was his own sister that had been arrested for the murder. She went quite pink with excitement when I told her. We became very pally during our little gossip, and presently she insisted on going downstairs to make me a cup of tea. I begged her departing back not to hurry.

I made a rapid search. In his desk letters were carelessly scattered about. There were several brief messages in a large feminine script, simply signed O, or Yours O, to say that she expected him that week-end or that he was to expect her that evening or something of the sort. And there were some more urgent and effusive missives in a flowing handwriting, signed Tessie. I had no time to examine them then so I crammed a few into my pocket, in case they might come in useful later. In the compactum in his bedroom, hiding under a pile of shirts, was a small leather-bound volume. Inside, half the pages were covered in small, rather childish writing that was sweetly familiar to me. It was Judy's diary. That too I pocketed.

I glanced round the room. In one corner of the mirror was stuck a long strip of pink paper. I went over to look at it. It was a cheque for two hundred pounds made out to Terence Allen and signed by Judith. I whistled. That was quick work. And what on earth was it doing stuck in the mirror like that, as though it wasn't worth the stamped paper it was written on? Funny chap! Of course, with his right wrist broken he couldn't endorse it, but still that was surely no reason to leave it lying about. Maybe he was like his mother — careless. But what kind of a cad was he to soak his little sister for two hundred of the best? It was all I could do not to tear it down before returning to the sitting-room half a minute ahead of the little landlady.

Over the tea, I chipped her playfully

about her affection for Terry. How about his other girls? Didn't they put her nose out of joint?

No, she bridled, 'im and 'er understood one another.

I implied that when we had been buddies he had been a dashing Lothario. Well, he was not what you'd call fast, like the young men nowadays. 'E liked 'is joke and a bit of a cuddle, but he never went too far — well, not 'ere anyway, this being a respectable 'ouse.

And what about the young lady she had mentioned earlier? Wasn't that serious? Well, now, serious it might be. But who for? It took *two* parties to make a contract, didn't it? And Mister Allen was such a good-looking young chap that lots of ladies lost their 'eads over him.

He had written a lot to me about someone he called Tessie, I lied. Would that be the young lady in question?

Lor! she'd die of laughing. Miss Fane wouldn't 'arf be flattered. Why, Tessie was her age if she was a day. She'd never see fifty again, she'd warrant that much. Hard as nails and a face to match, but ever so wealthy, 'e said she was. 'E said she was rich beyond the dreams of Avarice — whoever she might be. (But she seemed to remember that that was the name of a little snippety actress he brought here once or twice.) It was just 'is fun to call 'er Tessie, daring-like, because she was so stern. Old Glumface would have been a better name for her. Nice 'e was to 'er, because she was aiming to set 'im up in business. Though what exactly, 'e never said . . . Yes, 'e *was* 'ard-up most of the time, but then young men mostly were, weren't they? Yes, she often let 'im run 'is rent on for a couple of months. No good being 'ard on a chap, even if it was your living, and he always paid up in the end.

'By the way,' I said. 'Didn't you tell me just now that he had broken his wrist? Did he go to hospital, or did his own doctor attend to it?'

'Oh, Doctor Sherriff, I expect; but I never arst him. I always say these hospitals . . . '

I let her run on for a while before I called it a day.

It didn't take more than a few minutes to locate Dr. Sherriff in the phone directory. He was out. But when I explained that I was a private dick, the receptionist girl was quite amiable. I only asked her one question, and it only took her a minute to look up the answer in the book. I was satisfied.

Curdie Baxter, I found, lived in the kind of boarding-house that styles itself a private hotel. He was not in, they told me, but they gave me an address in Acton where I might find him. Cursing mildly I drove there, and after some trouble found the place. It was a disused warehouse, where he was rehearsing some players in a curious surrealist scene. No one paid any attention to me. I leant against the wall at the back and watched. Since the actors addressed him as Mr. Baxter, I guessed that the dynamic little man in the centre of the improvised stage was Curdie. He didn't shout and rave or fling himself about the way some producers do, but his personality was forceful, controlled, and almost hypnotic. The play, or whatever it was, seemed pretty crazy to me. The scenery, too — well, it might simply be a lot of old planks and rolls of lino and sacking left behind by the last tenants in the warehouse.

Presently Baxter complained that they were mumbling and he retired to the far end of the warehouse, to where I stood, in order to hear how their voices carried. They all sounded as if they were worn out, he said crossly after a minute or two, and if they were they had better take half an hour's rest and recover.

At once the stage was filled with a subdued clatter. I intimated that if Mr. Baxter was free I would be glad of a word with him. Baxter, who had suddenly and astonishingly become a quiet and docile little man, said, Certainly, and Who was I?

'Bob Stone is my name, but I don't think that would mean anything to you. I've come on behalf of Miss Allen.'

'Oh yes,' said Baxter, and waited.

'Well, I suppose you've seen the papers? How she's been arrested . . . We thought you might have some helpful ideas or information. You see — '

'Arrested!' he echoed, and his bony

fingers bit into my arm. 'But I saw her yesterday afternoon. It's impossible!'

'You misunderstood me. I meant Miss *Judith* Allen, of course. Goodness, why on earth should Miss Antonia be arrested, she didn't have anything to do with it, did she?'

'You young fool! I know all about Judith. I was there when it happened. And if I had had any ideas or information I should naturally have told them before now. The whole thing is a complete mystery to me. I'm afraid I can't help you.'

'What a pity! Oh, don't go yet, please. I'm sure you can tell me more than that. Perhaps you can tell me whose idea it was, yours or Antonia's, to leave Judith to drown in Little Limpington Bay?'

'What the hell are you talking about?' he snarled. 'Who are you? And what are you driving at?'

'I've told you, and you weren't any the wiser. And I'm here, as I said before, to find out anything I can that might be useful to Judith Allen.

'I see . . . Well, I've already told you

that I know of nothing that would be of any use to you. Now, if you'll excuse me I must get back to the rehearsal.' He began walking away from me as he spoke.

Not a lovable character, and it was obvious that he lacked both money of his own and financial backing — else why this shoddy and inconvenient theatre. I didn't envy Antonia her life with him if they married.

On a sudden impulse I drove to the town hall that was not a stone's throw from the private hotel where he lived. I asked to see the records. Almost at once I saw what I had only half expected to see, and my heart jumped . . . Under yesterday's date was recorded the marriage of Curdie Baxter, bachelor of that parish, and Antonia Frederica Allen.

I climbed back despondently into the jalopy. Why so sudden? Having stalled her off for so long on one pretext or another, why had he suddenly changed his mind, or what arguments had she used to persuade him? And why the secrecy? Had it anything to do with the case in hand, or was I letting my imagination run away with me? Yet there *was* an instance . . . In the eyes of the law, a married person was not required to testify against his or her partner. More than once, I knew, this had proved an effectual way of sealing a person's lips. In this instance, it would be enlightening to know which had persuaded which into the marriage. If I could find out that, it might not be so very hard to find out why . . .

As I drove back to Elder Hall, I caught a glimpse of Olivia Fane pottering about in her garden in a pair of exquisitely tailored emerald green dungarees. It was six o'clock and a good time, I decided, for paying a social call. I leant over the gate and admired the garden audibly. Miss Fane turned and smiled at me, and then frowned.

'I can't imagine why anyone ever plants goldenrod. It's a beastly thing that grows like a weed and isn't even pretty to look at. It's simply choking out everything else in the garden,' she complained.

'There does seem rather a lot of it. Why don't you root some of it up?'

'I would if I could only get near enough

to it, but as soon as I get within reach of it I begin to sneeze my soul out.'

'May I do it for you?'

'Bravely spoken, young sir. You may. The spade is yours.'

I laughed and vaulted the gate.

Miss Fane leant artistically against an ornamental sundial and cheered on my efforts as I laid the plants one after another on the ground. When I had dug up half a dozen and was resting on my spade, she said that I had done enough and that I could now go into the house and get my reward — a cocktail mixed by her own fair hands, she said, stripping off her gardening gloves, or an iced beer.

The ice tinkled in the metal shaker.

'You're not very forthcoming, I must say,' she said. 'But I suppose if you won't tell me who you are I shall have to tell you. I don't know your name. But you're the young boy who met poor little Judy on the boat coming over and fell in love with her . . . What's the score?'

'Double-centre,' I said. 'How do you do it? Do you use a crystal, like Mrs. Allen?'

Her laugh tinkled like the ice in the shaker.

I snapped open the top of the beer-bottle, poured it foamingly into a pewter tankard, and settled down into a serious talk with her. She couldn't help being glad, though perhaps it was rather wicked of her, that awful creature Brady was dead and couldn't get his beastly claws on little Judy. Although she scarcely knew her, she had quickly become very attached to her, she was such a sweet kid. Then, too, Judy had rather a rave on her, Miss Fane admitted with a smile. It would have been too ghastly if that bigamist had managed to get hold of her. The odd thing was, that although she had nothing against the man, she had always disliked him, and she had warned Judy as well as she was able against him. Besides, Judy had not been really in love with him. It was a mere infatuation, hero-worship for an older man.

About that car of hers, I suggested. Oh, she had parked it at the back of Selfridges. And when she came out it had gone. Of course she had informed the police at once, and they had merely promised to do their best; a lot of cars were being stolen just then. Some gang, they supposed. We both agreed that it was very astonishing that it should have turned up two days later safe and sound with a dead girl in it in the Allens' garage. Utterly fantastic! No, she did not know the girl. She had heard since that she was the daughter of Millicent Allen's bailiff. Yes, she knew him slightly, the way one did know neighbours in the country. The Allens? Rather sweet people, though she was not really friendly with them. She had contacted them first through professional channels — Toni had designed some dresses for a play that had caught her eye. Then Toni had invited her down for a week-end and she had met Terry, who was really rather a lamb and had fallen for her with a bang. Sweet, but of course quite hopeless except as a playboy. He was grand to go around with, because he was handsome and amusing, and she had gone around with him quite a lot, she didn't mind admitting. But he had had a bad crush on her and it was the kindest, simplest way she knew in which to work it out of one's system. He was practically free of it now, she smiled, and although she was glad in one way she was going to miss his company.

I tipped back my head and let the cold beer go prickling, trickling down my throat.

'Have you met his future wife?'

'Oh, he's not thinking of jumping out of the frying-pan into the fire,' she laughed, 'even on a ricochet.'

'Oh, I'm so sorry. I naturally thought you knew that he's going to marry — er — Tessie,' I said comfortably.

She arched her beautiful, fine eyebrows. 'No, I didn't know. He never told me. And they say women are fickle. Well, well . . . '

'Gosh,' I said. 'Miss Fane, please don't go by me. I guess I got it wrong. I can be pretty stupid sometimes.'

'My poor lamb,' she said. 'There's no need to perspire so about it. If it piques my pride a little, that won't harm me.'

'Gosh, it's swell of you to take it that way!' With easy tact she let it ride, talking pleasantly of other things till I got a hold on myself once more.

We became pretty friendly. Presently she was asking me who I thought had committed the beastly crime.

'We know it isn't darling little Judy,' she said. 'And if the police are as stupid as to arrest her, it doesn't give one much hope that they'll be clever enough to track down the real murderer, does it?'

'I know. It's a terrible thought. But you know, one always somehow takes it for granted that a criminal is brilliantly clever, a sort of master-mind, but there isn't any reason to suppose that he is. Why should he be?'

'Except that he's evaded detection so far. Still, it's a comforting idea. And they're bound to let Judy out soon, aren't they? They can't have any real evidence against her.'

'God, I hope so,' I said gloomily. 'Unfortunately, I happen to have seen Exhibit A, and though I know that somehow it's a lie, I also know that juries the world over think an awful lot of circumstantial evidence.'

'Poor kid!' She looked awfully sad and sympathetic. 'It's ghastly, but I suppose we've just got to be patient. I wish there was something I could *do*. You'd tell me if there was, wouldn't you, Bob?'

'Sure,' I said absently. And then suddenly I sat up and slapped my leg. 'Why, there is something you can do to help, Miss Fane, if you really mean that.'

'Why, of course, I'd do anything to help Judy. Tell me what it is.'

'Listen,' I said. 'Did you know that Antonia and Curdie were married?'

'No! How absolutely extraordinary!' she said slowly, with a puzzled frown. 'Why are they keeping it such a secret?'

'That's what I would like to know. They were married only yesterday.'

'Curiouser and curiouser!' murmured Olivia. 'Rather an inopportune moment to have chosen, I should have thought.'

'I'm glad we see it in the same light. There is another unusual feature about it, too: the happy couple spent the bridal night about fifty miles apart. A trifle unfriendly, no? Moreover, I saw the bride

270

last night, and she was looking far from radiant. But perhaps that was because she did not like being separated from hubby so soon . . . Seriously, it does seem a little unnatural. I mean, why all the hurry, if you're not going to get together?'

'It's just a riddle to me, my dear. You don't think that perhaps — dear me, I hardly know how to put it — that there was some reason for a hurried marriage?' Olivia suggested.

'Madam, I'll excuse your coarseness. I'm no judge of those sort of things, but *I* think not. Be that as it may, this is where I want your help. Can you go around there and pump Antonia? I want you to be feminine and friendly. Call her 'Sister' and let down your back hair. You know what I want, get her to confide to you that she is married.'

Olivia grimaced doubtfully. 'Toni isn't exactly the confiding type. She doesn't go in for winsome girlishness, I'm afraid.'

'I'd rather gathered that. But that is what I want you to have a shot at anyway. Use your feminine guile. Try and discover which of them urged the other into this holy bond of matrimony. Will you have a shot at it?'

'I will. Because I'm madly curious to get the answer to this puzzle, myself, quite apart from doing it to help Judy. I suppose it *is* to help Judy, though I fail to see the connection.'

'Not your fault,' I said. 'You couldn't be expected to see the connection. You see, Brady's murderer requires an alibi for round about one o'clock, not three o'clock, as Judy thought. That's important, of course. Toni, for instance, has an alibi all right for three p.m., but nothing tangible for one. The same goes for lots of other people too, if it comes to that, but we simply must follow up every channel, do you see?'

She said she didn't. But it didn't matter. She also added that she liked me, and a lot more guff about being glad Judy had such a grand friend. I reckoned I'd stayed long enough anyway, so I tootled away. One way and another I was feeling pretty tired, but decidedly pleased on the whole with my day's work.

14

Death Strikes Again

When I was cleaning myself up for dinner, in my room at Elder Hall, I discovered to my annoyance that Tessie's letters were missing from my pocket. They were there all right when I left Terence's rooms. Where could I have dropped them in the meantime? If they were not in the jalopy, that meant I had lost them at the warehouse, Curdie Baxter's theatre, or else the town hall, or Miss Fane's. It would be too provoking if those letters fell into the wrong hands. I foresaw that more trouble could arise from that, and I cursed my carelessness.

All the family were seated round the table, except Judy, of course. I didn't want to think of what kind of a meal she was making. Terry was quieter than people had led me to believe he would be. But perhaps he had something on his mind; he looked thoughtful.

In the middle of the meal, Toni was called away to the 'phone. When she came back she glared at me malevolently, and then turned to Mrs. Allen and said it was Curdie; he would like to come down for a night or two if it wasn't inconvenient.

'I dare say we can lump him in somewhere,' Mrs. Allen said amiably, chewing her not salad.

'I can easily go down to the local, Mrs. Allen, if there's not enough room,' I said eagerly.

'Oh no, my child, you don't want to do that. We always manage.'

'If I didn't have only a single bed, he could share my room,' Toni said.

'Toni!' said Mrs. Allen, in the automatic voice mothers use to correct their offspring.

'Oh, it's perfectly all right, darling,' she said nonchalantly. 'He is my lawful spouse.'

'Toni, are you breaking it to me that you have married Curdie Baxter?' her mother asked sharply.

'That's it.'

'When?' rapped out Mrs. Allen.

'Now let me see . . . I know I was busy all Wednesday . . . and yesterday I . . . It must have been the day before yesterday. Yes, it was. I distinctly remember it now.'

No one laughed. Major Thompson looked puzzled, Terence was frowning, and Mrs. Allen was frankly displeased.

Toni seemed disconcerted for a moment.

'What, no good wishes? No cheers? No bouquets? No confetti? Can it be that my dear family disapprove?'

'My dear child, approval, and good wishes come before marriage, not after. You know how much I dislike underhand behaviour; you surely can't have imagined that your sly wedding would please me. And why all the mystery? Why did it have to be secret?'

Toni shrugged. 'It didn't *have* to be. We both happened to prefer it that way. I was joking about congratulations just now. Neither of us want that rot. What has it got to do with anyone else if Curdie and I decide we want to go to bed together? Curdie loathes all those barbaric rites that make people gloat over weddings. He says that if they realized what all that revolting symbolism meant they'd be sick. So we always swore that when we married it would be quite casually, without telling anyone about it or having any fuss. And we wouldn't have a honeymoon or any disgusting orgy of sensualism like that. I quite *expected* all my friends and relations to be furious when they found out. But, after all, it is our life.'

'Do you know, it hardly seems worthwhile marrying on those terms,' said her brother mildly. And I felt more than half inclined to agree with him.

Thompson, addressing Mrs. Allen, said, 'I tell you what I think, old lady. I wouldn't be a bit surprised if human generation ceased altogether in another hundred years or so. That is, if young people don't get over their self-consciousness.'

'Meanwhile, my poor boy is falling asleep at the other end of the line,' interrupted Toni. 'What am I to tell him?'

'Oh, tell my son-in-law to come by all means, if he thinks propinquity won't be too much for his ideals,' said Mrs. Allen.

'Not if you're going to be nasty.'

'No, we'll be resolutely normal, I promise, and not one festive drop of champagne shall you be offered.'

Toni stuck out her tongue vulgarly, and retired to the mellow privacy of the 'phone.

Mrs. Allen shrugged her shoulders, with a, The-girl-is-mad! expression arching her winged brows. 'These children!' she muttered, and apparently dismissed the matter from her mind.

After dinner, Olivia Fane drove over, as she had promised. It was nice of her to come. I had not expected her so soon.

And Toni seemed only too ready to escape from us all, away upstairs with her.

I didn't see either of them again that night, as I made an excuse to retire early. I had a lot of work to do, putting all I had learnt that day in focus. By the time I had finished I was ready for bed.

I don't know what time it was that I was half-aroused by the crunch and spatter of gravel as a car came up the drive, swinging its head-lamps' beam across my room. I supposed sleepily that it was Curdie, and turned over on my other side.

Then I was talking to Mr. Lockett, and he was telling me that he had discovered it was the Chief Constable who had killed Brady. He said if I wanted proof to go and ask Mrs. Garnet. And when I asked where I could find her, he said, Goodness, didn't I realise that she was Terence's landlady? The body was in the warehouse, he said. And when I asked whose body, he looked immensely cunning — and sinister. It suddenly dawned on me that somehow or other he was the criminal. But to my horror he read my thoughts and said that I was the murderer, he'd merely been leading me on in order to trap me. And he gripped me by the shoulder hard. The more I struggled and twisted, the deeper his fingers dug in. He was shouting at me. Shouting, and shaking me furiously.

I woke up abruptly. Broad daylight was streaming through the wide-flung windows. Curdie Baxter, in pyjamas and dressing-gown, was still pulling at my shoulder. 'For God's sake!' he exclaimed in relief, when he saw that my eyes were open. 'I thought you were never going to wake up. I thought maybe you were dead too. For heaven's sake hurry, man. Something's wrong, or I've got the wind up. The bathroom's locked, and there is no answer to my knocking. I don't want to scare the women. And you were the only person I could call on. You see, Terry isn't in his room.'

I thrust my feet into a pair of slippers, and glanced at my watch. It was five past eight. 'Come on,' I said, 'I'm ready.'

We ran down the low-beamed corridor to the bathroom. Baxter banged fiercely on the door. 'Hullo there!' he shouted. In the ensuing silence he turned to look at me expressively.

I say silence, but it wasn't really still. From behind the door could be heard the sound of rushing waters. And something else crept from behind the door too; a slow but steady stream of water worming its way through the gap at the bottom of the door and spreading darkly across the beige pile of the carpet.

'Hullo,' I yelled again, and peered through the key-hole. But the key was in the lock blocking the view. 'Come on,' I said to Curdie, wishing he was a bit heftier. 'Both together, when I say 'Go'.'

The corridor was too narrow to allow of a run-back, and we got what purchase we could from the opposite wall. Again and again we hurled ourselves on that door, hearing it creak protestingly against the assault of our united bodies. I began to think it would never give. I was aching all over and felt as though every ounce of breath had been knocked out of me. I was almost ready to give up, when the damned thing gave way and hurtled us spitefully into the bathroom, almost on to the body sprawling on the floor.

It was lying face downwards, one arm crumpled under it, but I could tell by the back of the fair head and the gay brocaded dressing-gown that it was Terence.

Both hot and cold taps were turned full on and water was cascading over the side of the bath. Terence was half immersed in it, and already it was lapping tepidly about my ankles and rushing boldly out now through the open door into the corridor. I stepped across the body, leant over the bath, and turned off the taps.

Curdie was just behind me, raising the skirts of his dressing-gown and his pyjama-legs above the water. I wondered, with that silly part of one's mind that notices trifles, whether the expression of distaste on his face was caused by the unpleasant sight on the floor or the clammy water soaking through his slippers. Then I bent down and gently turned the body over.

Although the body was warm, there wasn't any doubt that he was dead. His glazed eyeballs stared at me out of his distorted face. The water ran off his face in tiny rivulets and trickled into his open mouth. There was nothing handsome about him now; he looked horrible.

'He's dead, isn't he?' said Curdie in a muffled voice.

'I'm afraid so.' Something was clenched in his left hand that lay under him, and I was trying to see what it was without disturbing the position of the body too much.

'What do you think — ? I mean, how — ?' stammered Curdie.

'Here, hold him up a minute, will you? I want to get at his hand.'

'I'm awfully sorry, old chap. But I think I shall heave if I touch him. I really am sorry to be so useless. If there is anything else I can do — '

'Oh, go to hell!' I said tersely, not feeling that this was the time to indulge in lady-like sensations. However, I managed it alone by groveling on the water-logged floor and propping him on my own back. A piece of blue celluloidish stuff, about as thick as my little finger, jutted out of his left hand. I prised the fingers up a little way, far enough to see that the object he held was a tooth-brush.

I stood up. I was as wet now as the corpse, and my pyjamas clung to me soppingly. On the glass shelf above the wash-basin was an open tin of tooth-powder, branded with a well-known name. It was more than half full of a white, crystalline powder. I shivered, although the air was still warmly steamy from the hot water and very faintly fragrant with an acrid, almondy smell.

I said, 'Look here, I won't be a moment. Can you stay here without passing out? Don't let anyone come in, and whatever you do, don't let *anyone touch anything.*' I hurried away, unbuttoning my pyjamas as I went. I slipped them off on the threshold off my room, grabbed up my dressing-gown, and hastened off to the telephone.

I explained matters briefly to the police, and I heard someone exclaim at the other end of the line, and then promise to come along right away. I was relieved that they hadn't wanted to ask me a whole lot of foolish questions, for I didn't wish to leave Curdie too long, in case I found him in a faint or worse when I got back. But I didn't.

As I came down the passage I could see Mrs. Allen's great bulk standing on the threshold of the bathroom. She turned when she heard me. Her face was utterly blank. Then she put out her hands, and toppled over, very slowly, so slowly that I had plenty of time to catch her as she fell. I lurched under the weight of her. I felt like one of those ridiculous little comedians on the stage. I could feel my knees giving way. I shouted for Curdie but there was no response. This was absolutely crazy. Presumably he had passed out too. What was I supposed to do with her? Fat women, I thought irately as I tried to bolster her against the wall, ought not to faint, they ought to have more consideration. Then I saw Curdie hurrying down the passage towards me. I was furious, but it was no use being angry with him from behind a wall of fat.

So I merely said, 'Help me get rid of this. Take her heels. We'll try to carry her to her bedroom.'

Luckily it wasn't far, and we dropped her thankfully on the bed. I rang for the maid to come and attend to her mistress.

'Look here, Baxter,' I said. 'Didn't I expressly tell you *not* to leave Allen, nor to let anyone go near the bathroom? Damn it all, I wasn't gone five minutes. And yet when I came back you'd vamoosed, and in consequence, Mrs. Allen has had a fearful shock.'

'I say, I'm most frightfully sorry. I

didn't realise. But I was only gone a minute.'

'Yes, a minute too long. However, it's done now. The great thing is not to let it occur again. Would you mind going back there again till the police come. I want to stay with Mrs. Allen.'

'The police?' Curdie raised his eyebrows. 'You're taking rather a lot on yourself, aren't you? Sending for the police, and ordering your elders and betters about.'

'Would you like to take charge?' I offered sweetly.

'God forbid! I never cared to poke my nose into other people's concerns.'

Then perhaps he wouldn't mind obeying those who had taken charge and weren't afraid of taking full responsibility, I suggested. He trotted off.

Mrs. Allen opened her eyes, and stared at me blankly. Her face twisted up.

'My boy . . . my boy . . . ' she moaned. 'Who killed him . . . ? Oh, Terry!'

'What makes you think he was killed, Mrs. Allen?' I interposed swiftly.

'Killed?' Her lids fluttered upwards. 'I

don't know why I said it. Was he? Was he . . . ? Oh, Bob, promise me you'll find out who killed my boy, my darling boy . . . ' Tears were running freely down her white cheeks and she made no effort to stem the flow. The maid brought brandy neat in a glass, and she drank it down as though it was water. Then she waved the maid away, rocking gently to and fro in her grief. I thought it best to let her cry.

'She'll never get over it,' murmured the maid to me, in dispassionate tones. 'Idolised him, she did. There wasn't nobody meant as much to her as Master Terry.' She cleared her throat and looked at me out of the corner of her eye. 'What 'appened, sir? Did he kill himself?'

'I gather you wouldn't be altogether surprised if he had.'

She looked smugly down. 'I know what I know.'

But whether she knew much or little, or of what importance it was, I could not wait to discover then, for I heard a bell ring and then voices in the hall, and I hurried down to greet the police and conduct them to the scene. I was pleased to find that Baxter was still there. I sent him away. Incredible though it seemed, it was only twenty-five past eight now. It seemed hours since Baxter had awakened me.

While the police surgeon bent over the body, I narrated to the sergeant what had taken place. In the background a tall young policeman wrote it all down.

The water had soaked up somewhat but the floor was still wet, and the doctor carefully turned up his trousers above his knees before he knelt down to make the examination.

'Of course, the fact that the deceased has been lying in hot water all this time naturally makes a difference to the body temperature. Rigor-mortis may have already set in, but I don't see that I can be expected to judge very precisely when he met his death.' He glanced up at me irritably as though it was my fault somehow.

'Judging by the amount of water that had overflowed by the time we broke in, he can't have been dead more than five or ten minutes. If I am correct in assuming that he, himself, turned on the bath water just before he died. Death, I suppose, was instantaneous, and must have occurred while he was cleaning his teeth. I hope I'm not speaking out of turn, but very likely the tooth-paste — ' I broke off.

'Yes?' said the sergeant encouragingly.

'It's gone,' I said stupidly. 'It was on the shelf there. Damn it all, that's not reasonable. I was gone hardly any time at all.'

'Really! But what were you just going to say about it?'

'Listen,' I said. 'There was an open tin of tooth-powder on that — '

'Just a minute, you said tooth-paste before.'

'Oh, well, paste or powder — I was speaking generically. Actually, it was a powder, a white, rather crystalline powder. And there was a slight depression in the centre where the brush had been pressed firmly down in order that the grains should adhere to it. A faint smell still lingered in the air then, a bitter, nutty odour. I didn't need to investigate the powder to guess what it was. You will be able to confirm my guess, Doctor, that Terence Allen died of cyanide poisoning.'

'He seems to know a lot about it, doesn't he?' remarked the doctor to the sergeant. 'I wonder he thought it necessary to drag us poor folk from our breakfasts.'

I was remembering Curdie's sudden absence from his post as guard, his unexplained absence. And I remembered, too, that Mrs. Allen had been there alone, for how long I did not know. Curdie hadn't seemed surprised that Terence was dead, had seemed rather to expect it. While his mother had at once jumped to the conclusion that he had been killed. True, there had been rather an outbreak of sudden death and disaster. Yet they all rather took it for granted in a way. I wondered what Toni's reaction would be. One thing I had time to be glad about, that Judy was not in on this. Partly, because she had had quite enough horrors for a lifetime, and partly because I hoped it would help to prove her innocence. If Terry's death had anything to do with the other two, then surely the fact that Judy was safely tucked away behind bars would help to establish that she was not involved in any of the catastrophes. I hoped she had not had time to become too fond of her brother anyway.

The police surgeon rose from his knees and rolled his trousers neatly down again. 'I'll give you my report as soon as possible,' he said snootily to the sergeant, pointedly ignoring me. 'Better get the body sent down, too, so that I can make a proper examination.'

When he had gone, the sergeant turned to me.

'Where can I question all these people? Do you know how many there are in the house at present? I don't know what's come over our little place, I'm sure. It's what they call a crime-wave, I suppose. Of course, it's all in the way of business for me, and I was rather pleased at first, I don't mind admitting, thinking it would be a bit of promotion for yours truly; but having all this, one right on top of another, you know, well I don't like it, makes me look a bit of a fool. Not that it's really my responsibility any longer, it's the Chief Constable's, and I don't expect he's going to feel too happy about it when he has to tell the Yard. But I'm running on . . . Well, I suppose the first thing to do is to have a look for that tin of tooth-powder you say is missing. It's a rum go, isn't it? Have you any idea where it might be?'

I shrugged. 'In the furnace by now, most likely.'

'Just run along and have a look,' he said to the constable who was still standing discreetly to one side, scribbling industriously. Obediently, he folded up his notebook and ran along.

The sergeant and I walked down to the library for the examination. He settled himself in a lordly fashion behind the desk in the corner and rang the bell.

A little maid called Lucy answered it, and although she patently knew nothing about it, the news had drifted below-stairs and she was green with terror.

How had she heard about it? Oh, Martin, Mrs. Allen's personal maid, had told her. Had she noticed any of the family or their guests downstairs, in the kitchen, or near the boilers, for instance? Lucy shook her head. And then looked more terrified than ever.

'What is it?' asked the sergeant.

'Ooo, I don't know, sir. I don't know if I ought to mention it.'

'You'd better let me be a judge of that,' said the sergeant genially. 'If it's anything that doesn't concern us we'll forget all about it.'

'I forgot for a moment. But I did see Mr. Baxter, sir, coming up from the cellar.'

'This morning?'

''Bout a quarter past eight, sir.'

'And what made you think there was anything odd about it? Did he look flustered or something?'

'Oh no, sir. Nothing special, I didn't notice. I just thought to meself, now whatever has he been up to down there?'

'So I expect you popped down and had a look, eh? Notice anything?'

Lucy blushed and looked impressed. 'Yes, sir, I did. But I couldn't see he'd done anything. 'Cept he left the light on, careless-like.'

'Well, thank you — er — Lucy. I don't suppose it was important, but thank you all the same. And — er — I shouldn't talk about it, you know, just in case.'

'Ooo, no, sir,' she agreed readily. 'I'd never sleep easy in my bed again, for fear I should wake up and find my throat cut from ear to ear . . . Cook says she's going to leave. It's no better than a charnel-house, she says.' After which sinister remark, she departed.

The cook, who came next on the list, knew nothing but had plenty to say, and the sergeant had quite a job to get rid of her. The second housemaid, too, was soon dismissed.

Martin came next, prim and knowledgeable. She was not surprised. She had her own theories about it all. *She* didn't think he had been killed. Why should anyone want to kill him, a nice, harmless, young chap like that? No, in her opinion he had done himself in. Always getting himself in trouble one way and another, he was. Most people didn't know that, but she knew, because her lady confided in her. No, she didn't have any secrets from Martin. And as the young master used to mostly go to his mother when he was in trouble, she, Martin, could tell them as much about it as anyone. Of course, the mistress spoilt him, always had done, and that was what Mr. Allen had never been able to abide; jealous, he'd been, especially when Master Terence turned out to be — ah, well, it didn't do to speak ill of the dead, did it? Martin crossed herself piously.

Well, to her way of thinking it was like this. Things had altered considerably now that Mr. Allen had died and left all his money to the young Miss. It put everyone else in a bit of a hole. And it wasn't much use him coming to his mother again, if he was in trouble, for this time she wouldn't be able to help. There you are! What would he go? Face the music? Not him. He hadn't been brought up to that. No; likely enough, if he was faced with something nasty like a stiff term of imprisonment, he'd take the easiest way out. Well, that was her idea, and if it was of any use to us gentlemen we were welcome to it.

We thanked her, sighed, and sent her away. The sergeant looked at me questioningly. I shrugged, grimaced, and shook my head.

The young constable came in, carrying gingerly on a half sheet of paper a charred and buckled but still recognisable tin.

He nodded to me affably. 'Quite right, sir. In the boiler. Wonderful how you knew.' I wasn't so sure I liked the way he said that, but I let it pass.

He deposited it on the table in front of his superior, who turned it over curiously with the tip of a pen.

'Not much to be gathered from that, now. Not so much as a fingerprint left on it,' he said contemptuously.

'No matter. It's told us the chief thing,' I said consolingly.

'What's that?'

'Why, that it did contain the cyanide. Else why the hurry to dispose of it?'

'Oh, that,' in a tone that warned me not to score too often. 'Who shall we have in next . . . ? I rather fancy a look-see at this Baxter bloke.' He turned to a clean page in his notebook.

Baxter came in, sat clown, took out a cigarette and offered the case to us. Not the least disconcerted by our refusal, he lit his own, and waved to the sergeant permission to commence.

'You'd better tell this in your own way, I think.'

'There really isn't much to tell. Toni invited me here yesterday, and I drove down as soon as I'd finished work. Got here about one-thirty, I suppose. Toni was waiting up for me. We had a bit of a snack and then we went to bed . . . Well, that was that. When I woke up this morning I thought I'd nab the bathroom if I could. So I trotted off and found it locked. I had passed Terence's room on the way, and as his door was open I was able to see that the room was empty, so I feared the worst. I mean, I took it that he had beaten me to the bathroom. So when I found the door was locked, I gave him a shout. There was no answer and I thought perhaps he hadn't heard above the sound of the running water, so I thumped pretty fiercely on the door. There was still no reply. But I didn't begin to get really anxious till I noticed the water creeping under the door and realized that it was overflowing. Then I got the wind up. And the only thing I could think of to do on the spur of the moment was to rouse the only other man in the house. Which I proceeded to do. Well, the rest he can tell you,' he indicated me with a nod of his head.

'You simply know no more about it than that?'

'Absolutely.'

'Were you surprised to see that Allen was dead?'

'Well, yes and no. I realized that something had gone wrong, he'd been taken ill or something. But, of course, I was astonished when I saw he had been murdered.'

'Oh, you saw that he had been murdered. That was very smart of you. How was that?'

'Oh, I don't think there was much doubt about it, was there?' He turned to me for confirmation. 'He looked so very dead, somehow.'

'But why should he have been killed?'

Curdie sat upright and stared at us. 'Yes. Exactly. Why? A point that had not as yet penetrated my thick skull. I wonder . . . '

'Then you haven't any idea who might have done it?'

'I? Oh no.' As much as to say, who am I to presume to trespass on police terrain.

'Then what made you remove the tin? Sheer whimsy?'

'What tin?' he said languidly.

'This one.' The sergeant lifted its paper covering and poked it slightly towards him. 'Just an old tin that once contained tooth-powder you see, and has now had its whiskers singed in the furnace of life, so to speak.'

Curdie rubbed one thumb gently against the other, gazing at the tin with a blandly disinterested eye.

'Means nothing to me. Afraid I can't help you.'

'No, I didn't really think you would be able to. But perhaps you can explain to us why you went down to the cellar,' the sergeant suggested nicely.

I saw his eyes flicker behind his spectacles. His mouth opened.

'You were seen,' explained the sergeant.

'I'd — I'd rather not say,' Baxter faltered out at last.

'Really, Mr. Baxter,' said the sergeant disgustedly. 'You put yourself in a very peculiar position — invidious. Here you are, left alone with a corpse for five minutes, with explicit instructions not to leave it on any account. And what do you do? The minute you find yourself alone you dash off to the cellar. Why? Oh, you'd rather not say . . . You must see what a position that puts you in.'

'Perhaps he went down for a quick bracer,' I suggested smilingly.

'Ha, ha!' Baxter laughed politely. 'A jolly good notion. Wish I'd thought of it. But, no, it wasn't that.' He studied his fingernails. 'As a matter of fact, I — er — thought I'd better break it to Toni — about her brother, you know. And I happen to know that she often goes down to her dark room in the cellar and does some developing before breakfast. So I thought she might . . . but, of course, she wasn't there.'

'I see. And when you came up you left the light on by accident.'

'Did I? Perhaps so. I was in a hurry, you know. Didn't dare be gone too long. As it was, I got into hot water from this young man for letting poor Mrs. Allen come upon her dead son unawares.'

'And also for letting someone get away with that very important tin. At least, I would have scolded you if I had known,' I said.

He looked sheepish. After a little more talk we let him go.

'Well?' said the sergeant.

'Hooey! He was putting on an act.'

'That was my impression. But why, do you suppose? What *was* he up to in the cellar? Did he get rid of the tin? And why?'

'Well, I've got a bitsy notion at the back of my mind, but it needs confirmation. I'll keep it till then, and let you have it later, if it's any good. Do we take Antonia Baxter next?'

'Antonia *Baxter*?' he raised his brows.

'Yes, didn't you know?' I explained the state of affairs.

Antonia looked very pale and strained beneath her tan. She nodded briefly, as if she could not bring herself to speak. The sergeant opened proceedings with a gracious little speech, sympathising with her loss and regretting the necessity of bothering her with questions at such a time, but —

'Let's take it as read,' she cut in. 'I'm feeling like death warmed up myself. And the sooner this is over the better. Fire away.'

She couldn't tell us much. She had the idea that whoever had done it must have been outside the house, a stranger, one of Terry's friends. He had such very funny friends. No, she had no logical reason to suppose that, except that before now he had got mixed up with some very queer people.

'Do you know how he was killed?'

'No. How?'

'You haven't — er — seen him then?'

She shook her head decisively. 'I couldn't bear to.'

'Did you by any chance go in the cellar this morning . . . ? No? What time did you wake up?'

'I slept late.' The tip of her tongue

slipped over her dry lips. 'The maid woke me at eight-thirty with the . . . news. I — I went along to see Mother, but there wasn't anything I could do. So I got dressed, and then you sent for me.'

'We'd like to see Mrs. Allen. Do you think she is up to it?'

We interviewed Mrs. Allen in her bedroom to facilitate matters.

She was lying on a couch, wearing a flowing, white, negligee affair. On a fragile table beside her was a bottle of Courvoisier, half-full, and a glass. She was not crying but was lying quietly, her face composed into lines of sadness. Her silvery fair hair was swept loosely back, waving off her face. She looked rather impressive in her grief.

She clasped her hands together as we came in and said, 'Oh, Inspector, what have you found out? Please tell me what you know. My poor head feels absolutely bursting. My poor darling boy.'

The sergeant bore his rapid promotion remarkably well, merely blushing slightly. He understood her feelings. He sympathised. He only wished that he had something to tell her. Unfortunately, these things were rarely so simple that they came to light immediately. She could best help them to a solution by telling them anything that she knew — however unimportant it might seem.

She swore that she didn't know a thing about it, not a thing. If he was in any trouble he had not confided in her.

Yet she had sensed right away that he had been killed, hadn't she?

She was afraid that she couldn't remember what her impression had been in that first numbing instant, and after there had been nothing but the horror of it . . . If she had taken it for granted that he had been killed it must have risen up out of her sub-conscious mind, where all sorts of peculiar thoughts were supposed to propagate, from no power of one's own? After all, he *had* been murdered, hadn't he?

The sergeant slid a pencil back and forth between his fingers. Mrs. Allen's maid, Martin, for instance, had jumped to the conclusion that he had taken his own life. One's impressions were not always reliable.

She raised herself on one elbow to declare earnestly that never, never would her boy have done that. Positively not.

Her opinion was welcome, intimated the sergeant. By the way, when she had stood at the bathroom door, had she happened to notice whether a tin of tooth-paste stood open or shut on the shelf over the wash-basin?

She had seen nothing but her poor dead boy, lying twisted on the floor, staring up at her. She buried her face in her hands.

We waited uncomfortably. Respecting her grief. There was a tiny knock at the door and it opened without waiting for an answer. Major Thompson came in, walking almost on his toes, and wearing a suitably shocked expression.

He went straight to her, ignoring us.

'Milly, my dear,' he said. 'I've just heard.' He put his hand gently on the top of her bent head. 'Poor old girl,' he said.

She jerked her head away and glared up at him, her eyes like slits of molten steel.

'Take your hands off me,' she hissed. 'You dirty swine!'

He stepped back, astonishment written all over his face.

'I say, old lady! What's up? You're distraught . . . '

She was on her feet now, facing him. 'So this is your revenge! You devil, I'll get you for it, I swear, if it's the last thing I do.'

She was utterly transformed. From a grief-stricken, sorrowing mother, she had become in an instant a kind of harpy, with fury shooting out of her finger-tips, her eyes; the very ends of her hair seemed electrified with her passionate hatred. No wonder Thompson looked alarmed.

'Now, Milly, old girl, calm down, do . . . You're overwrought. I can quite understand how you feel. Why, it's only a few weeks since I lost my own girlie — '

'Stop him! *Stop* him!' she shrieked to us, clapping her hands over her ears madly. 'I can't bear it! I shall kill him, I warn you! Take him away! *Make* him go away!'

'Oh, I don't mind going, if she doesn't

want me.' He looked at us appealingly, 'But, you know, I can't understand it. It's not like her. Does she imagine I had something to do with it? I didn't. Oh no, absolutely not, I assure you . . . '

I conducted him outside. I was serious, sympathetic, affable. I left the sergeant to tackle a hysterical Mrs. Allen — perhaps it *was* cowardly of me! — while I went downstairs with Major Thompson and salved his injuries.

15

The Web Tightens

The doctor's report came through: Terence had died of cyanide of potassium poisoning, administered orally. Now, cyanide of potassium is not the sort of stuff you can go in and buy half an ounce of at the chemist. It is so very deadly that it is pretty difficult, almost impossible to get hold of. There were certain legitimate excuses for procuring it, such as destroying wasps' nests, but otherwise . . .

When the questioning was over, I wandered down nosily into the cellar. I was just on the prowl, to see what I could see. Antonia's little photo-gallery and dark-room I found very interesting. The dark-room was not a groping untidiness at all. It was very well planned, with everything neatly ranged on shelves. I let the pinpoint of light from my pocket-flash wander over the bottles and tins. One of them was labelled in large, rough capitals, CYANIDE POTASSIUM. It contained a white powder that gave off a sharp, distinctive odour of almonds, bitter almonds. I carefully replaced the lid with my handkerchief-wrapped fingers. The torchlight shone on a few crystalline grains spilt on the shelf near the tin; as though someone had removed too much and in returning it to the tin had clumsily spilt a little in their haste. Yes, I found the cellar very interesting, if not very surprising.

As I came up out of the trap-door — remembering to switch off the light — I saw Olivia Fane walking in at the open front door. When she saw me she ran towards me.

'It's too *awful* . . . I've just heard . . . I *had* to come over; but what am I to say to the poor woman? I've never heard of anything so dreadful in my life. Is there *anything*, anything at all that I can do . . . ? Do tell me if there is . . . And only last night we — ' her small white teeth clamped down hard on her nether lip and she turned her head away.

'It's awfully decent of you, Miss Fane, I don't believe there is anything. Of course; sudden death does cause an upheaval, but there is Curdie Baxter — '

'He was so young — '

'And I have just 'phoned the solicitor, and very likely he will be over soon to see to that side of affairs. Though I don't suppose . . . '

'I'll have to see Millicent. It's the neighbourly thing to do. But what on earth can I say to the poor soul? It's ghastly! Everyone knows how she adored him; I was fond of him myself . . . ' She put her hand on my sleeve. 'Bob, they're saying — they're saying that Terry was murdered . . . ' Her eyes held the question her lips dared not frame.

I nodded.

'Oh, God,' she muttered. 'Oh, my God, it's as if there was a curse on them all. It isn't possible to have such tragedies, one after another like that, is it? . . . Oh, *why* are we just standing here? Why don't we *do* something? What are the police doing? Are they all asleep or mad?'

'They are proceeding according to their

normal routine,' I said. And at her furious gesture, I added, 'But what is the use of scurrying about in circles unless you know what you are up to and have a plan? It's sheer waste of time. The police do their best in the way that they have proved to be the best.'

'Oh, men are so *slow!*' she cried in a voice that broke with the weight of tears in it. 'It needs a woman's mind — I'm going up to see Millicent now.' And she broke away and ran up the stairs.

'Olivia! Just a minute,' I called, and hurried after her. 'I shouldn't be in too much of a hurry to see Mrs. Allen. She's got a sort of *thing* about people just now. She's almost crazy, you know. Doesn't know what she's saying half the time. But she's liable to run at you and accuse you of murdering Terence. It's rather alarming, you know. Poor old Thompson, he was in a state about it. Genuinely hurt. And she might have hurt him physically, too, if we hadn't got him away at once.'

Olivia closed her eyes and screwed up her face in a grimace of pain. 'Oh, Bob, how terrible it is!' She was standing so close to me that I could see the incredibly fine texture of her smooth milky-white skin, against which her lashes lay in black silk crescents, tipped with gold. She really was very beautiful. I couldn't help being aware of that. Far more beautiful than Judy. But then — she wasn't Judy. A faint fragrance clung to her, a bitter not unfamiliar scent, like crushed ivy. Unusual, and yet its strangeness became her. In some subtle way she reminded me of ivy, although she was not what one would describe as the clinging type.

She opened her eyes suddenly and stared at me. 'You don't think Millicent could have had some reason for taking up that attitude about him?'

'I don't doubt for an instant that she had. But where does it get you? You can't just go around accusing people without proof. Not even as bluff, you know.'

'He had a grudge against Terry. And I can't pretend that Terry absolutely doted on him. He's a low creature, in my opinion. Not as bad as that outsider, Rex Brady; but just as much of a bounder in his own way.'

'Yes, he doesn't seem really popular round here, and now his prop and mainstay has turned out to be a broken and extremely sharp reed. But what would he gain by killing Terry? I mean, you don't murder people because you dislike them . . . unless, you happen to be married to them of course.'

'I suppose so,' she said thoughtfully. 'I hadn't really thought of that angle. Why should he kill Terry?' she mused. 'Look here, I'm going to try and find out . . . No, I won't tell you what I'm going to do. But I'll be careful. I won't put my foot in it, nor will I put him on his guard. Not if I can help it . . . No, Bob, I want to *do* something. If I can only do *something* to help, I shall be so glad. You've no idea what I'm feeling like inside.' She put the back of her wrist against her forehead and smiled, a sad little three-cornered smile . . . I tried to figure out why I associated Olivia in my mind with the school-lab . . .

In the afternoon Mr. Lockett and I went over to see Judy. Though I was reluctant for her to hear any more bad news, I had much rather break it to her myself than let it come lightly from a stranger's lips. I hoped I wasn't being optimistic in imagining that I didn't seem a stranger to her. Anyway, she had to know some time.

There was something horribly pathetic in the gallant smile she gave us, and the cheery greeting that rose to her lips.

'What's new?'

'My dear,' said Mr. Lockett, and took her hands gently in his. 'Not good news, I'm afraid. But you will be brave.'

Her eyes pleaded with him.

'Your brother — '

'Oh no!' she cried. 'Not dead? Terry! And he was so alive!' She turned to me. '*Why* did I ever come here? There's been nothing but bad happen since I arrived. Bob, take me away! Bob, darling, *please*.' She was shaking all over and trying not to cry.

'Sure,' I croaked. 'Sure, honey. Be glad to. Y'know that. Get you out of here in a day or two now. I promise, sweetheart. Please don't cry, Judy, it tears me open inside. Just stick it for a day or so, and we'll have cleared it all up. Isn't that so?'

Mr. Lockett nodded.

'Suppose you don't? Suppose I have to stay here forever? Suppose you *can't* prove my innocence? I'm scared, I tell you; I'm scared to death. I sit here all day and think about it, and I dream about it all night. See? I think I'm going crackers.'

I made my voice come out harsh and casual. 'Pull yourself together, Judy. Fancy letting yourself go all to pieces like that! As though I would let you down. I'll let you in on something, my lass. I could have got you out of here any time. I could have established your innocence if I had wanted to. But it happened to suit my purpose to keep you here. Out of harm's way, do you see? Don't glare at me like that, I mean it. Don't you see, there's a killer going around loose, and though he doesn't seem very particular who he rubs out, I don't think there is any doubt that you head the list. And while you're here he can't get at you — that is something he positively cannot do. You may not care for the service here, you may not admire the view; but at least a cell is considerably more spacious than a coffin. And that seemed to be the alternative . . . Am I forgiven?'

She thrust out her underlip sheepishly, and gave a reluctant salute in acknowledgment. 'O.K., I'll stick it,' she said. 'No half-baked Yankee is going to take a poke at me.'

'That goes better. I've always *heard* that the British bulldog hangs on till the end, and that nothing will shake him off or daunt him!'

By the time we left she was quite cheery, quite reassured that she would soon be free to leave the past behind her. And I had told her the truth.

We had expected Mrs. Allen to keep to her room that evening. But, oh no! She had an idea which she insisted upon carrying out. Everything about her seemed wilder and vaguer than usual: her dress and hands fluttered ceaselessly, and her eyes were wild and staring in her big white face. Her very distraction made her appear more ethereal. She wanted to hold a séance, with everyone present, in fact, she insisted upon it. Somebody remarked that there was no medium. But Mrs.

Allen did not care. She did not *demand* materialisation. She did not even expect to get in touch with her darling boy; not first go off like that, things weren't as straightforward as all that on the Other Side. But there was no reason why we should not try to contact a spirit and induce it to answer a few simple questions. We might discover something *very* helpful that way.

Curdie Baxter violently disapproved of the idea and was not afraid to say so. Miss Fane rather timidly brought out that she was scared to death of anything spooky, and could she be left out of it, please.

But Mrs. Allen was adamant. *Everyone* was to participate. The more the better. And there was nothing at all to be afraid of, the spirits could not harm one, and would not if they could. In any case, she only intended to try simple table-rapping. If that was successful, they could experiment with more complicated methods later.

Eventually, she chivvied us into the dining-room and seated us according to some mystic order of her own in a circle about the polished mahogany table, hand just touching hand. The curtains were pulled; the lights extinguished.

We sat in this order. To the left of Millicent sat Mr. Lockett, then Major Thompson, Miss Fane, myself at the bottom of the table opposite Mrs. Allen, then Toni and her husband.

'Now,' commanded Mrs. Allen. 'Kindly all join with me in singing, Abide with me. This is to promote unity of spirit and thought, so please everybody concentrate . . . reverently. La!' She gave us the note, and off we went all the way through the hymn.

In the ensuing silence the clock ticked loudly. The minutes seemed very long.

'Oh, my God, how long do we have to endure this farce?' demanded Baxter, breathing hard..

'Please, Curdie, be good,' whispered Toni the peacemaker.

Silence once again. Miss Fane made a curious little sighing noise once or twice. I realized sympathetically that she was trying to suppress irrepressible yawns. My own head was beginning to nod in spite of me. It was so warm and dark — so dark.

A terrific thump in the very centre of the table jerked us to alertness. It sounded as if a very solid object had been dropped on the bare mahogany.

Mrs. Allen said, 'Who is that? Is it a friendly spirit?'

Silence again, and at last a thump.

'We are all friends here. Can the spirit answer some questions for us! We are in trouble. We seek your help. Will you help?' Mrs. Allen's voice was clear and plaintive. 'One knock for yes and two for no?'

Thump.

Mrs. Allen cleared her throat. 'Was — was my boy murdered?'

We waited. But neither one knock nor two came to enlighten us.

'Are the spirits still with us?'

They signified that they were by taking another hearty crack at the table.

'Will they help us to discover how my boy met his death?'

'They' thumped assent.

'Was he murdered by the same hand

that struck down . . . Elsie Thompson and Rex Brady?'

'*Alias* Averil Day and Graham Garnet,' interposed Curdie, *sotto voce*.

My end of the table raised itself very slowly about six inches off the ground, remained hoisted up a few seconds, and then dropped down with a thud and began rocking violently to and fro. It seemed the spirits could not make up their minds on that point, or else could not come to a decision. The table subsided with a couple of hiccupping jerks.

'Is the — the murderer present among us now?' Mrs. Allen's voice trembled slightly.

A distinct and uncompromising thud.

Someone drew in his breath sharply.

I say, this is awful rot, isn't it?' said the Major appealingly.

'I agree,' said Miss Fane. 'I don't believe we should meddle with such things.' Her chair scraped backwards.

'Don't break the circle!' called Mrs. Allen sharply. 'Keep still.'

'Well, I don't know that I'm liking it

much either. Mother, Let's stop it . . . And there's a spirit blowing down the back of my neck, and I'm going to have an awful crick in it tomorrow.'

'For goodness' sake, Toni, don't mock at the spirits.'

'All right, it's a draught. But I honestly think we ought to stop this,' there was an undercurrent of urgency in her tone.

'You're a coward, Toni. Don't you want to see your brother's murderer unmasked, *whoever it may be?*'

'Yes; but need it be done in this way? It seems quite useless to me. You still lack proof; it's only a kind of bluff.'

'And it isn't very pleasant to be here in the dark and to think that you may be sitting ne — in the same room as a murderer,' chimed in Miss Fane's gentle voice.

'Oh, you women! Illogical and superstitious! You've not an atom of proof that the murderer is in the room . . . Well, ask the lawyer. He'll tell you that spirit rappings aren't proof of anything, not even of spirits,' said Curdie impatiently.

But I was tired of kicking the table.

'All the same,' I heard myself say quietly, 'I don't think anyone need doubt that the murderer is one of us in this room right now.'

Major Thompson said, 'And what the deuce do *you* know about it, anyway?'

'I believe I know all about it now.'

'Very clever of you, I'm sure,' said Baxter sarcastically. 'And why haven't you informed the police, may I ask?'

'They will be informed in due course,' I promised.

'Waiting for proof,' murmured Toni. 'And who the hell *are* you, anyway?'

'Mr. Lockett will vouch for me, if you care to ask him. I am a private investigator, an employee of the Fidias Agency, New York.'

'I thought there was something fishy about you,' I heard the Major mutter knowingly.

'And might one inquire,' said Toni sweetly, 'who called you in?'

'I was called in on this case by the late Mr. Rex Brady, especially to safeguard Miss Judith Allen. Well, I did safeguard her, but unfortunately at the expense of three other persons . . . one of them my own client.'

'Why should Brady have called you in? I don't get it.'

'On the principle of set a thief to catch a thief, I'm afraid. He was after Judith himself. He had a pretty good idea that one of you here would have a shot at killing her for her money. He gauged your scruples pretty accurately. And he decided to get in first. He had a fast-working brain, had Mr. Brady. Directly the news came though that Allen had left his money to her, he cabled our agency in New York to keep our tabs on her from the word go . . . If I'm going to tell this story, Mrs. Allen, may I have the light on for it?'

Mrs. Allen gave me the O.K. and I groped my way to the switch, turned it up, and returned to my place at the table. I waited, watching them all blinking at one another in the sudden light.

Olivia leant forward. 'One thing I don't understand at all. What connection can there be between Brady and — Terry? I can vaguely see why — why they should try to kill Judith, and I can see why they would need to get Brady out of the way if he was going to marry her. But where does Terry come in on this? Or was he killed accidentally in mistake for someone else?'

'That is an interesting point, Miss Fane. It might have been like that, but somehow I don't believe it was. You shall have an opportunity of judging for yourselves, however. Is everybody quite comfortable?'

16

The Web Becomes a Noose

'The thing that had me bewildered for a while was a certain confusion of style in the type and execution of the crimes,' I began. 'Now, I like to get the psychology of my opponent all mapped out. And if I know how his mind works I have a pretty good chance of being a jump ahead of his next move; that's the detective's aim, anyway. But these crimes were puzzling in their conflicting angles. Sometimes I thought I perceived certain unmistakable feminine touches, and yet again, there were lapses no woman would have made. It took me a long time to figure out that there were *two* minds at work, one masculine and one feminine. And they were working, not against each other as I first thought, but in cahoots.

'Now I looked around for a couple who might have some interest in working together. Including Judith, there were nine people involved — well, ten, because I counted in Mr. Lockett. He might have partnered Mrs. Allen. Very likely, when one looked at the evidence with an unbiased eye, for the crimes bore just those signs of daring and speed coupled with the vagueness and carelessness one would expect from such a partnership. — Yes, there was Mrs. Allen and Mr. Lockett and Major Thompson and Miss Fane and Judith and Elsie Thompson and Rex Brady and Terence and Antonia and Curdie Baxter. Ten of you, five couples, and capable of almost endless combinations when one came to examine it. I don't want to weary you with all my activities. I'll just give you a brief résumé of how the crimes occurred and when.

'I was hired by Mr. Brady to bring Judith Allen safely across to England without her knowledge. We travelled over on a different boat from the one they expected, and in consequence they went to meet us at one port while we arrived at another. That avoided any nasty hold-ups or car accidents. Bear in mind that at this date I had not the least idea what I was supposed to be shielding her from. We arrived here in good order. Only she would not let me bring her all the way up to the house. There was nothing for me to do about it except give in gracefully. I didn't think she could come to harm in that short distance. What did happen, you know. An engine running in the garage drew her attention. She went in and found a dead girl in the car. She lost her head and ran out into the road and began screaming. It can't be pleasant to have a corpse fall on top of you.'

The Major fidgeted with his tie.

'But it was a little odd that Mr. Brady should have been so on the spot. Maybe he was waiting for her. Maybe he knew what was in the garage and guessed what her reaction would be. We know that he wanted to trap Judith into a bigamous marriage, and to that end he would have used any weapons that came to his hand. If it had been worth his while he would not have hesitated to murder Elsie Thompson in order to scare Judith into believing she was in danger of her life.

The girl was sufficiently like Judith to be mistaken for her by someone who did not know either of them well, and she had been got up rather carelessly to make the most of that likeness. She was dressed in the American style, but her clothes were actually English, and no more than a cheap imitation of Judith's. That pointed to Brady more than ever, because he did not really need her to be taken for Judith, the likeness would not be meant to deceive anyone — but Judith, and she would only be asked to accept it as proof that what he said was true. Yet if Brady had done it, why hide the body in the garage? Why not drape it artistically on the front steps, for instance, to create a far greater impression? And again, why hide it in that particular car, which had been stolen a couple of days earlier in London, but it was owned by Miss Fane, who did not omit to warn the police of her loss. Why should Brady have so laboriously stolen Miss Fane's car in London in order to kill Elsie Thompson in it down here? Unless he wished to place the guilt on Miss Fane, and then why not have directed suspicion more thoroughly by replacing the car in *her* garage? And why should he wish to throw the guilt on Miss Fane, who was not a member of the family? Why not have used any stolen car, if it had to be stolen at all? It was too much of a coincidence to suppose that he had not known it was Miss Fane's. So altogether there was something uneven there, a piece of jig-saw that simply would not fit.

'When I came down a few days later and saw my employer for the first time, I was disagreeably surprised. Especially when I found that Judith scarcely knew him, but had a pronounced rave on him already. I hinted to her that all was not for the best, but I had so little to go on beyond vague suspicions that I'm afraid my warning was not of much use.

'Events seemed to be running in Brady's favour, proving that he was correct in his assertion that someone was trying to kill Judith. Someone shot at her one night when she was taking a moonlight stroll. She nearly drowned, because no one bothered to warn her about the tide. Luckily and unluckily, Brady turned up like a movie-hero in the very nick of time and saved her. Wasn't it natural for her to fall into his arms in the circumstances? Her nerves were shaken, and she believed his story. It was more or less true, as it happened. She agreed to marry him secretly as soon as possible. Unfortunately for him, she was too much in love to keep the secret to herself. She told it in confidence; but it spread like the wind, and before she knew where she was, the banns were being published. Poor Brady, he must have been scared when he found out. He realized the danger he stood in. The only thing that surprises me is, knowing that, that he was so easily misled by the forged note inviting him to the hut. Judith recognized that her note was a fake, but she went all the same — the plucky kid! — hoping to discover the guilty person.

'But this crime was too well planned for any mistakes of that kind. With great daring and good timing, it was carried through without a hitch. One or both of the criminals had an excellent knowledge of psychology. Judith walked smack into the trap they had laid for her. And she acted exactly as they had foreseen she would act. In fact, they were in a fair way to disposing of two birds with one stone, and getting Judith neatly out of the way as well as Brady, by causing her to be convicted of Brady's murder. A pretty plot, indeed!

'So Judith was arrested. And that was where I stepped in. I didn't care for the idea of her battling by herself to prove her innocence from behind bars. I got down to it right away.

'This is the way I reconstructed the crimes, finally,' I said. 'Very likely the whole plot sprang into being when one of them ran across Averil Day and noticed the slender resemblance between the two girls, a resemblance which they saw could be heightened quite easily. And Averil Day was an actress. I guess that was all they knew about her. They thought it was all they needed to know. They asked her if she would be willing to take a job off the stage, impersonating someone for a few days. They probably dangled a nice fat sum before her eyes, and she was her father's daughter. She was told little enough, except that she was supposed to be an American heiress, but she must have guessed it to be something rather unsavoury. Anyway, it was arranged. Possibly the man gave her ten pounds to buy herself some American-style clothes, if she needed them.

'Well, the car was stolen, and huddled away in some friendly and uninquisitive garage, with altered number-plates. Then, on the day, one of them departed to Liverpool — mistakenly, as it happened — to waylay and assassinate Judith there and then and dispose of her there, conveniently far from home-territory. That fell through, as you know, because we took the other route.

'The other one drove Averil Day down here. It must have been on the way down that Averil asked where she was going. And when she heard it was Elder Hall she would have exclaimed with surprise that that was where her father worked. That must have been an awful moment for the criminal. What to do? It was necessary to do some fast thinking. If they turned about and drove back to London, the whole thing would be ruined, the warning would go out that Judith had never arrived, and most likely the missing body would be found and eventually the deed traced to them. That was hopeless. Yet it was too risky to let the girl attempt to go through with it, for her father would be bound to recognise her and then, either the fat would be in the fire, or he would need to be brought into it too, and there would never be a moment's peace for any of them. No, there was only one thing to do.

'I don't like to think of that poor girl riding to her doom, while her murderer sits beside her cold-bloodedly planning her death. It was all worked out with lightning speed. The car was driven into the garage. 'Wait there,' says the murderer gaily, 'I'll fetch a drink to brace you up before your ordeal.' And off went the murderer to mix the deadly cocktail. I cannot say what all the ingredients were, but the chief one was paraldehyde. A drug I discovered only today that the murderer took against insomnia. In thirty seconds Averil was knocked cold. That was all there was to it. The engine was left running. The doors and windows were closed. The fumes were left to do their deadly work, while the murderer departed to prepare an alibi.

'It was an elaborate plot wasted, but the situation had been saved. As soon as possible accomplice number two informed accomplice number one. The main problem was still unsettled, but there was nothing to prevent them having another shot. Then, while they were debating ways and means and waiting for the fuss to die down, they learnt the shocking news that Brady was going to cut them out by marrying her. That stirred them up. They realized that Brady would rush the wedding through, and that meant they had to work fast if they wanted to be in time.

'Accomplice number one in Town, who is no mean forger, fakes up a couple of letters purporting to be from Brady to Judith and vice-versa, and dispatches them to accomplice number two down here, who sees to it that they arrive at their destinations at the right moment. Accomplice number one also contrived a neat little note for Mrs. Garnet, with letters cut out of a newspaper, telling her that her husband was up to his tricks again. You see, he knew that much about Brady. That was supposed to reach her and bring her down on the *day of the murder*, but unfortunately that part of the plan miscarried, because Mrs. Garnet was away that day and did not receive it till the following morning. She came down then at once. But it was too late to pretend that she could have already told Judith of this, and thus given Judith a motive for killing him . . . which was what they were trying for. However, that couldn't be helped. To resume then, accomplice two went up to Town to provide an alibi for them both, while accomplice one drove down here in a very fast hired car, strolled into this house, with an excuse ready on his lips if he was seen, removed the revolver from Terence's room, slipped the back way up Breem Hill, killed the unsuspecting Brady who had been decoyed up there two or three hours before Judith was due, ran down again, replaced the revolver for Judith while they were all sitting at luncheon, and back to Town as quick as hell. Judith takes the planted gun — from which *one* shot only has been fired — and puts her fingerprints all over it. And everything goes according to their plan. Yes, they must have felt very satisfied when Judith was arrested. They must have thought all their dreams were coming true. They were both so greedy, so luxury-loving. And yet, although she loved him so, she was too selfish, or perhaps too wise, to marry him without wealth behind them. Foolish people! As though money was something solid! Yet perhaps she did love him in her selfish, possessive way. She wasn't going to let anyone else have him, anyway.

I looked round at them. They were all listening intently enough now, hardly daring to breathe. 'I am indebted to Mr. Lockett for telling me some of the family history. Without that valuable information, I doubt if — '

Mr. Lockett leant forward. 'Might one

inquire what it was I said that put you on the track?'

'The whole thing was most enlightening. I'm very grateful, but particularly for the information that Mr. Allen — to his bitter shame — had to cover a cheque for his son . . . to save him from prison. I think that is correct, is it not, Mr. Lockett?'

Mr. Lockett bowed his head. Mrs. Allen was staring down at her plump white hands lying on the table. Antonia stammered through pale lips, 'Are you trying to tell us — to tell us — that Terry was the — did the — '

'You knew he had forged, didn't you? You knew he could imitate writing; he must often have done it for fun as a kid. You can't be very surprised,' I said.

'I know. But he had broken his wrist. How could he?' she pleaded.

'Oh, that! The oldest gag in the world. He stuck on a bandage and pretended he had broken his wrist; then he wrote the letters, drove down, and shot Brady with his revolver; and only broke his wrist *after* all that business was concluded. That alibi always seemed a little too tight to me. And when I found Judith's diary in his rooms, I knew I could break it. Why else should he take her diary except to copy her writing? He didn't dare risk not breaking his wrist at all, in case it came to a show-down. But that meant he had to go to a doctor to have it set properly. Naturally, the real date that the wrist had been set was down in the doctor's records. Four days later than he had pretended. Oh yes, Terence was desperately in need of money. He had borrowed two thousand pounds on his expectations, and then he found his expectations were nil, and he had not even the money to pay the interest on the loan. And his accomplice was as corrupt and cunning as himself. She knew as well as he did what they were doing; she helped to plan the murders, she helped to execute them. Hers was the hand that actually killed Averil Day. And while Terence was murdering Brady, she provided an alibi to satisfy the inquisitive. I wonder if either of them felt a qualm of conscience when they shouldered their guilt on to an innocent girl! I doubt it. Neither of them appeared to possess any moral sense whatsoever. Profoundly egotistical, their whole lives were devoted to the supreme task of satisfying every want of their own loathsome little egos . . . Ah, that was the trouble! It was all right while both of them wanted the same thing. But the moment came when their wishes directly conflicted. What happens then? What happens when an irresistible force meets an immovable object?'

Major Thompson tugged at his moustache nervously, as what I was saying filtered in.

'You don't mean to say, old boy, that Terence was mixed up in this murder? Why, it's incredible! I mean — '

'Yes, *you* believed Mrs. Allen had killed your daughter, didn't you? And, of course, the way she reacted to your tentative accusation did nothing to dispel that belief. But, you see, she didn't dare slap you down because *she* had a horrible fear that Terence had done it. So, although she was desperately hard up, she kept you dangling on a string as far as your little attempt at — Is blackmail too harsh a word for the truth . . . ? Yes, you knew your son through and through, Mrs. Allen. Well might you tremble. And you loved him; that was what made it so bitter.'

I sighed. Mrs. Allen was crying very quietly, her hands over her face. Mr. Lockett patted her shoulder, and the Major fidgeted sympathetically.

'Go on,' said Curdie. 'For God's sake, let's get this over.'

'She killed him. She took some cyanide of potassium out of the tin in Toni's darkroom, that she uses for developing, and substituted it for his tooth-powder. So very simple. So very sure. The rest you know. You recognized that it was cyanide almost as soon as I did, Baxter, didn't you? And were you in a stiff breeze! You immediately jumped to the conclusion that your bride had killed her brother — why everyone always suspects the worst about the people they love, I cannot imagine! You determined to protect her at all costs, so at the first opportunity I gave you — which was very careless of me

— you rushed it downstairs and replaced it in the tin; thereby making yourself an accessory *after* the fact.'

Curdie gnawed his lip bitterly. But Toni smiled, not a whit offended at being taken for a murderess by her husband, and I heard her whisper, 'You darling.' Under the table their hands joined.

I could feel Miss Fane's big eyes on me anxiously. I smiled reassuringly, and put my hand on her wrist.

'Crushed ivy . . . an unforgettable smell . . . Couldn't place it at first. Then I remembered paraldehyde. Was he killed without warning? Or did you go to him and directly accuse him of treachery? Did you show him Tessie's love-letters which I left on your divan? Did you plead with him? Did he attempt to deny it? Did he make specious promises to you?'

'I don't know what you mean! You're mad!' she cried, pulling her wrist away.

But I held her firmly, and even laughed a little, reproachfully. 'Why, Miss Fane, what kind of a detective do you take me for? It was so very simple for you to slip down and remove some of the contents of

340

that tin, after your little chat with Toni. I don't suppose anyone would have thought it odd if they had seen you going to his room to have a talk with him before you took that decisive step. They were used to you. You had been his mistress for quite a long while, hadn't you? That was the trouble. He was tired of you. But you were far from tired of him. An impulsive nature yours, Miss Fane. You never think before you act. Those letters don't mean a thing, they're from a crazy, repressed, old woman, whom he would never have married in a thousand years. Why should he, when he had gone to all that trouble to provide himself with a fortune? It must rile you bitterly to think you killed him for nothing — '

She was on her feet now. She swung her free hand and caught me fair and square on the jaw, shouting, 'You filthy swine, perhaps that will shut your mouth! It wasn't for nothing. He taunted me for supposing he would marry me. Why, he said, should he marry, and share the money? He'd been using me as a catspaw, secure in the knowledge that I could not split on him without involving myself. He never intended to marry me, he said — not he. He was laughing at me . . . I tell you I'm *glad* he's dead. Glad, glad!'

Her voice rose to a shriek, and her sharp, pointed nails tore down my face like fiery needles. Her face was vixenish, hideous. She was using her feet, too, in a furious effort to break free. I shouted to Mr. Lockett to unfasten the door.

The tall young constable was waiting patiently on the threshold. He came stolidly across and tapped her on the shoulder.

' . . . for your arrest,' he said. 'And I have to warn you . . . '

I helped the constable get her away, with Mr. Lockett following behind us. The room seemed to contain nothing but an astonished silence as we left it.

I wanted to go down to Garthurst right away and free Judith as I had promised. There were certain formalities to be gone through, but I knew dear old Lockett would hurry that along as fast as he could.

I waited in the police station, fidgeting, while Lockett wrestled with the intricacies of the law. And then at last

Mr. Lockett came back and said she was waiting for me, and I could go right along. I didn't need telling twice.

She was waiting in a kind of ante-room where they keep witnesses prior to examination. It was empty now, except for the two of us.

I said, 'Gosh, Judy!' and stood there holding her hands. We stood there, blushing and smiling stupidly at one another.

'I'm glad you came, Bob,' she said at last, the words coming out in a little rush. 'I've got a terrible lot to thank you for, haven't I?'

'Aw, shucks, it was nothing. I came down — I thought I'd just some down to say good-bye.'

'Good-bye!' she echoed. 'Surely you're not *going*, Bob! I thought — '

'I don't *want* to. I've got to get back to my job. I've been recalled. They want me on a case.'

She pulled her hands away from mine. 'Yes, I forgot. You never told me you were a detective.'

'I couldn't very well, in the circumstances.'

'No,' she agreed frigidly. 'You could hardly tell me that you were only making love to me because it was part of your job. I quite see that. I didn't take it seriously, don't worry.'

'You're trying to make me out a rat,' I said hotly.

'No, no. I'm *tremendously* grateful to you. Which reminds me, I wish you would tell me what your fees are. I'll make make out a cheque for your professional services to me.'

'Judy, that's downright rude. You know darn well that I wouldn't take a cent from you.'

She laughed lightly. 'Bob Stone, you're never going to pretend you did it for love.'

'Oh, even a snooper has his feelings, you know,' I sneered. 'It would be nothing to you to pay my fees; and you'd like to be able to dismiss me from your mind as easily as that — and cheap at the price. But any charity in this racket comes out of my pocket not yours, little lady lucre.'

'Charity means love really,' said Judy vaguely. 'Did you know that?'

'Well, that's all right, too. You want me

344

to say I love you, don't you? You hate to think I was pulling your leg on the boat coming over. Well, I wasn't. I *do* love you,' I said angrily. 'Everybody seems to know that except you.'

Judy's smile was sweet. 'It's so much better to be frank . . . And what are you going to do about it? Forget all about me in your next case, I suppose.'

'I'm going to kiss you good-bye and walk out,' I said, and took her quickly in my arms, clamping down on her mouth before she could protest. Her slender body was pliant in my arms and her lips were somehow soft and yet firm.

Her eyes were brighter than sapphires. 'I'm sure there must be a law against kissing in a police station,' she said dreamily.

'A very beautiful police station,' I reminded her. 'I would not be a bit surprised if when you came by here tomorrow there was only a fairy ring in the grass.'

'Idiot,' she said fondly.

I sighed. 'I wish I didn't have to go so soon.'

'Go!' she exclaimed. 'You can't go now. Why, I thought you loved me!'

'I adore you, I worship you,' I said, and further words to that effect. 'But it has to be like this.'

'But if people love one another — '

'*Do* you love me, Judy?' I said eagerly.

'Oh, my glory — men are so *slow*! I'm practically proposing to you and you ask me if I love you. In fact, I will propose to you, if you like,' she offered generously.

I shook my head. 'I can't marry you, darling.'

'Don't tell me you're a bigamist, too!'

'No. But I'm not a fortune-hunter, either. Sorry.'

'Don't apologise. You love me for myself alone, don't you, Bob? *I* know you'd love me just as much if I wasn't an heiress?'

'Sure. But folks'd think that I — Judy, I'm not a bit ambitious for wealth and society and all that sort of rubbish. I should honestly loathe to marry a rich girl and feel that I never need work again, and could spend the rest of my life lounging on Palm Beach — '

'Excuse me interrupting your recitation, dear. But you are labouring under a misapprehension. That sweet little Mr. Lockett has just explained to me. It seems the Will has been proved now, and they figure out that the reason Father left everything to me was that there was practically nothing to leave. He lost nearly all his money before he died, they say, and it simply wasn't worth while dividing the rest, so as I was his favourite he left it to me . . . Objection sustained?'

'Objection over-ruled,' I chortled. 'You angel!'

'Go on, then.'

I kissed her. 'Go on,' she repeated, when she could talk again.

'Oh, I see! . . . Dear Miss Allen, will you marry me and make me happy ever after?'

'Oh, Mr. Stone, this is so *sudden!*' she cried, and flopped into my arms with her eyes tightly shut, just as the door opened cautiously to disclose Mr. Lockett's withered face. He beamed.

'How very gratifying,' he remarked, 'to find that despite all this modern veneer the tender sex still retain their finer feelings. A swoon is such a sign of delicacy in a lady ... ' He was rapt in admiration.

But I didn't care, for I had Judy in my arms, and that was heaven enough for me.

BACKGROUND FOR MURDER

Shelley Smith

In a psychiatric hospital, the head doctor lies dead — his skull smashed in with a brass poker. Private investigator Jacob Chaos is called in by Scotland Yard to investigate. But there are many people who might have wished harm upon Dr. Royd: the patients who resented his cruel treatment methods; the doctors who harboured jealousy of his position; even his own wife. With Dr. Helen Crawford as the Watson to his Holmes, Chaos must untangle the threads of the mystery . . .

THE LIBRARY DETECTIVE RETURNS

James Holding

Former Homicide cop Hal Johnson now works as 'library fuzz' — spending his days chasing down overdue books, stolen volumes, and owed fines. He doesn't miss life in the fast lane. But his police training and detective instincts still prove necessary in the bibliographic delinquency division. For such apparently innocuous peccadillos on the part of borrowers often set Hal on the trail towards uncovering greater crimes: fraud, theft, drug-smuggling, arson — and even murder . . .

DEAD MAN'S PAIN

Valerie Holmes

A man being pursued collides with Nicholas Penn. Assuming his pocket has been pilfered in the scuffle, Nicholas also gives chase. But the stranger fails to see a horse careering down the road, and is trampled by the animal, seemingly mortally. Later, though, Nicholas discovers that the man was no thief — and still lives. Mystified, he is determined to discover the truth behind the 'dead' man's pain . . .

MORE SECRET FILES OF SHERLOCK HOLMES

Gary Lovisi

Five untold tales of the great detective. In the first, Holmes chronicles to Watson a strange event at a freak show years before he met the good doctor. The second sees Watson throwing a birthday party for his friend — but danger lurks among the festivities. The detective and the doctor play golf at St. Andrews, and then are invited to Paris to solve a most perplexing art theft. Finally, Conan Doyle's Professor Challenger meets the duo, who arrive in the hope of preventing an attempt on his life.

THE HUNTSMAN

Gerald Verner

Superintendent Budd is faced with one of his toughest assignments in separating the strands of mystery that grip the village of Chalebury: a series of robberies perpetrated by the burglar known as Stocking-foot; sightings of the ghostly Huntsman; and the murders of a villager and a local police inspector. Interweaving with these is the suspicious behaviour of a frightened young woman who lives in a large dilapidated house with one elderly servant. Is there a connection between all these crimes and other oddities happening in the tiny village?